GLASS LAW

Daniel and Will Glass were on opposite sides of a corrupt and mercenary law, one a dedicated peace officer, the other an innocent fugitive from so-called justice. With courage and determination they stood together against a powerful group of businessmen who were trying to seize power in Eagle Spring.

Countering violence with deadly reprisals they set out to end the brutality spreading from Eagle Spring to the Ozark Mountains.

GLASS LAW

Daniel and Will Glass were on opposite sides of a corrupt and mercenary law, one a dedicated peace officer, the other an innocent fugitive from so-called justice. With courage and determination they stood together against a powerful group of businessmen who were trying to seize power in Eagle Spring.

Countering violence with deadly reprisals they set out to end the brutally spreading from Eagle Spring to the Ozark Mountains.

GLASS LAW

by

Caleb Rand

Dales Large Print Books
Long Preston, North Yorkshire,
BD23 4ND, England.

British Library Cataloguing in Publication Data.

Rand, Caleb
    Glass law.

    A catalogue record of this book is
    available from the British Library

    ISBN   1-84262-005-3 pbk

First published in Great Britain by Robert Hale Limited, 1999

Copyright © Caleb Rand, 1999

Cover illustration © Prieto by arrangement
with Norma Editorial S.A.

Published in Large Print 2000 by arrangement with
Robert Hale Limited

Dales Large Print is an imprint of Library Magna Books Ltd.

Printed and bound in Great Britain by
T.J. (International) Ltd., Cornwall, PL28 8RW

1

The Killing of Moss Trinkett

Anxiety and fear gripped the clients in the River Bend Saloon. Whiskey and cards were pushed aside as cowboys and gamblers turned towards the three men at the bar.

William Glass stood very still, his left hand hanging close to the stock of his revolver. Through long black hair, his dark eyes were concentrating on the man facing him: Moss Trinkett.

Daniel Glass stood to one side of his older brother and, like Will, his hand was close on his gun. It was one of their father's matched .44 Smith & Wessons.

Will's voice pierced the thick atmosphere of the saloon. 'Trinkett, there's a bead missing from that necklet you're wearing.'

He placed a small stone bead on the bar. 'I found it where you shot my father. I can shoot you here, or in the street. Make your choice.'

Trinkett made a grab for the big Paterson Colt he carried across the front of his stomach. But he knew he was too late, and too slow. No one saw Will Glass move his left hand, or the bullet that tore into Trinkett's chest.

'Second mistake Trinkett.' Will's mouth hardly moved.

Trinkett's eyes froze, and a rill of crimson sliced his lips. His body jerked, then he pitched forward in a lifeless heap.

Will swept the bead into the spit and sawdust. Under a table, someone moved his hand, and Dan levered back the hammer of his revolver.

'I'll shoot the first man that moves, then I'll shoot someone else.'

A floorboard creaked, and at the rear of the saloon Carver Hayes stepped into view. He was the proprietor, with the tight frock-coat and fancy cravat. He took in the Glass brothers and the stunned faces of his customers. Then he walked over to Trinkett.

'Who's responsible for this?' He toe-rolled the body with the tip of his boot, and looked impassively at Will.

'Me, Carver. You can tell Sheriff Lummock that I'll find the others and give *them* a chance too.'

A grin spread over the gambler's face. 'Lummock's the law in this town. He's very jealous of his authority, and if there's killing to be done, he likes to do it. He'll regard this as a murder.'

Will took several steps backward. 'Trinkett drew first. Everyone here saw it.' He turned to the men who sat fearful in the saloon. 'Keep very still, gentlemen, move nothing. Hands flat on the table where they can't get into trouble.'

Matched closely in height and feature, the brothers backed through the door and swung into their saddles. They galloped up Main Street, but nothing came at them, only a spotted mongrel, viciously snapping at the ponies' heels.

'No one's following,' Will said, as they passed the outlying clapboards of the cow town.

'They've got time,' Dan shouted back, 'and they'll conspire to say you murdered Trinkett.'

The brothers eased their ponies to a trot, and Will half smiled at his brother. He leaned, and punched Dan in the leg. 'I was pleased to see you, kid. How come you're home? You haven't been kicked out, have you?'

If Will Glass felt any grief at killing a man, he failed to show it.

With a shake of his head, Dan said, 'No, I had a letter from Dad telling me about the trouble he was expecting. He busted himself getting me to West Point. I should have got here sooner. It might have made a differ-ence.'

Will pulled the brim of his hat down tight across his forehead. 'Yeah, maybe, Dan, but

I doubt it.'

The two riders passed through a narrow rock-lined gully that led to their home at the Horse Creek. Dan unsaddled his pony to browse amongst the sedge, and Will led his into the barn. He stared at the Ozarks that still glittered white in the dipping sun, then followed Dan to the ranch house.

A short, stocky figure greeted them, and Will said, 'Curly, this is my brother, Daniel. Dan, this is Curly. He's from Tennessee: been working with us for the last three months.'

Curly looked tough, but he had a back deformity that Dan couldn't help noticing. Curly saw his reckoning eye, and faced him front on to lessen the effect. With a direct look, he challenged the man who appraised him, but only saw the suggestion of a smile.

Dan said, 'Pleased to meet you, Curly,' and offered his hand in friendship.

Will turned toward the house. He was looking for the ageing gun-hand who, years past, had sought retirement and seclusion at the ranch. 'Hensa should be around some-where; he'll be pleased to see you, Dan.'

Dan put his hand on his brother's shoulder, 'What's going on here, Will?'

Hensa stepped from the veranda that fronted the house. He nodded in quiet, genuine pleasure, then turned into the open doorway.

In the ranch house the four men sat around a table, and Will explained their father's death to Dan. 'I was crossing the Piney looking for mavericks. I heard gun-shots and saw a rider, but he took to the higher ground through the pines. I found Dad with his horse standing over him. He'd been shot in the back. Two bullets from a rifle.'

The nerves at the back of Will's neck twitched with emotion. 'I tried to go after the rider, but lost his trail beyond the timberline. It was late when I came back, so Curly rode to tell the sheriff early next morning. You can imagine the help we got from Lummock. That's when I decided to bring in whoever shot him.'

Daniel muttered something about 'bring in', and Will looked up sharply. He got up from the table, walked to the open doorway, and looked to the darkening sky. 'Seven or eight days ago I went back and found something the sheriff hadn't. It was that blue bead. Moss Trinkett's Cheyenne ornament.'

By Curly's look, Daniel could see that he didn't fully understand. 'The Glass family own the Horse Creek Ranch. We're in a valley, and the Piney runs along the eastern border. About ten years ago, Goose Parker bought a tract of land, below the flats. But there's a five-mile bluff that cuts off the river from the ranch. He had to drill, 'cause there wasn't enough water for a herd. Not long after, he changed the existing brand to GP, his own initials. From then on, we all called it Goose Pond.'

Will turned from the doorway, and continued with the story.

'Soon after that, the Creek began losing cattle. It was easy for Parker to change our

C brand to a GP.' As Will spoke, he drew his toe through a glaze of dust to illustrate the change. 'All he had to do was work the P into the C. About a year later, Lummock was elected sheriff, then Carver Hayes opened the River Bend Saloon. There's nothing much for a hundred miles, so's plenty opportunity to work the town. It was a gold mine from the start. Shortly after this, an Easterner called Thomas Feigh arrived, and opened the bank. It was badly needed, and it was ranchers' money that made it a success, although most of them didn't care much for Feigh. Our old man noticed that with the exception of Parker's ranch, almost every acre south of the border was heavily mortgaged. Goose Pond is the only ranch inside five hundred square miles that makes money in spite of depression and drought. Dad helped out the smaller ranchers with our water, and that's what makes Thomas Feigh an unhappy banker.'

Curly sat and nodded. Dan remained seated and placed his revolver in front of him. He unhinged the frame and idly turned the cylinder. 'Feigh, Lummock, Hayes and Goose Parker are a sort of mutual society. They've crushed most of the smaller cattlemen by foreclosing and calling in loans. But they're stymied, as long as the Horse Creek controls the water.' He snapped up the barrel of his gun. 'They've tried to force us out by rustling the cattle. It's a strong group; they control everything. Eventually the old man got hard pressed, and had to take on a promissory.'

Will turned back towards the land beyond their ranch. He looked into the night towards Eagle Spring, and spoke bitterly. 'They knew he'd pay back the money. They knew him too well. So they shot him.'

Curly had been listening intently to the brothers. He sniffed hard before he spoke. 'How was them murdering your father any use? You're now the owners. I can understand the sheriff not chasing after the man he'd hired to do the killing, but...'

Will carried on. 'Yes, Curly, the Creek is

13

ours but we haven't much chance of keeping it. That loan's a lot more than we can raise, and they know it. They stole most of the breed stock, and you've probably seen there's less than fifty saleable head.'

Curly grinned and shuffled his feet awkwardly. 'I could help you. I've got money, had it for some time. It hasn't bought me much.' He looked sheepishly at Will. 'It's a long story, but you don't have to go to the bank. How much do you need?'

Dan and Hensa looked at Curly in surprise, and Will shook his head. 'Thanks, Curly, but I hadn't reckoned on borrowing. Dan was right. Hayes'll scheme to get me charged. The only witness I've got is my younger brother, and I think he's got his doubts.'

Dan smiled thinly. 'No, Will, I saw what happened, but it'll make no difference. Carver Hayes will testify against you. I wouldn't be surprised if there's a warrant out for your arrest right now. Paying off the loan won't make any difference.

'What will you do, Will?' Curly asked.

Will strolled outside. He sat on a wooden bench, and called back through the door, 'I'll stay here, and wait for Sheriff Lummock.'

Curly followed him out onto the veranda. He looked serious. 'What's to stop me bidding for the Creek? From what you say, you'll have to sell up.'

Hensa spoke softly to Dan. 'Interesting.'

Curly looked inside. 'I'm not much of a hand with guns, Hensa, but I can read some, and count. I'll raise any bid they make.' He bunched his large strong hands and turned back to face the open range.

Far off, a column of riders was outlined black against the night sky. Changes in landscape were part of Curly's watchful nature, and he'd seen them. 'Visitors. About a mile away.'

Will muttered grimly. 'It's the sheriff. I don't think I'll wait after all.'

Dan put his hand on his brother's shoulder. 'I'm sorry, Will. I don't blame you

15

for killing Trinkett. I just wish...' His words hung in the night air.

Will grinned kindly. 'You just wish it was different. Curly, if you're serious about this land, get a big gun. Hensa will show you how to use it.' He snatched a coat, and walked towards the back door. 'Don't worry about the sheriff, it's me he wants. And he knows what I'll do if any harm comes to you, or this ranch.'

The three of them watched Will disappear into the barn. Within minutes, he was galloping north. Hensa and Dan sat thoughtful on the steps, and Curly was inside, stomping with vengeance and retribution.

2

The Arrest of Joseph Church

Sheriff Lummock slid from his saddle, and Dan and Hensa stepped back onto the veranda of the ranch house. The big man came up the steps, and extended his hand in greeting. 'Daniel. I heard you was back from that smart army college.'

Dan hesitated a moment before shaking Lummock's hand. 'It's West Point, Sheriff. What brings you to the Creek so late?'

Lummock laughed. 'I reckon you know, boy. You was there with your brother when he murdered Moss Trinkett.'

'Murdered?' Dan repeated the word very carefully.

The sheriff ignored it. 'I know *you* didn't do the shooting, boy. I've got a warrant for

17

your brother's arrest. We trailed him here, and I'm not arguing the case. Where's Will?'

Dan shrugged. 'No idea. He left a while ago.'

'I hope you're not hiding him somewhere, boy. Under the bed maybe? That'd be a serious interference with the law.'

Dan looked straight at Lummock. 'If he was anywhere near, you wouldn't be standing here.'

Again, Lummock ignored Dan's provoking. 'Will should have come to me when your father got shot. Goddamn it, there wasn't a shred of evidence.'

Dan snapped back at Lummock. 'Will showed the evidence to Trinkett. That's why he went for his gun. It was self-defence. As Will said at the time, *second mistake*.'

It was enough for Lummock, he was losing the initiative. He took off his hat, and wiped the crook of his arm across his forehead. He looked at Dan and appeared to relax a little. 'The town's growing fast, and needs a deputy. Forty dollars a week, and full board. With your education an' all, you know there's no future for you here.'

'I'll do it for forty dollars a month, Sheriff, because right now that's an awful lot.' Dan turned his back on Lummock, and looked at Hensa. 'And from now on, the sheriff will call me Deputy, or Mr Glass.'

Lummock was surprised. 'What makes you so sure of that?'

'Because if you call me "boy" one more time...'

Hensa nodded approvingly.

The sheriff was aware of the financial troubles that touched Horse Creek Ranch, and his reasoning slipped. 'There's a reward of five hundred dollars to bring your brother in.'

Curly drew air through his teeth, and Hensa grunted loudly in disgust.

Dan gave no sign of his feelings, but thinking quickly, he said, 'That's generous of the town, Lummock, or would it be Hayes's money? I can't promise to catch Will, but as a lawman, I'll try.'

Lummock said, 'Taking the long, broad view makes sense.'

Less than ten minutes after the sheriff and posse had gone, Curly was angry and confused. 'Why? I'll give you that money. You don't have to go after him.'

Dan shook his head, sensing Curly's allegiance.

'I'm not going after Will; I've got something else in mind.' He pushed his hat into Curly's face. 'I hope Lummock fell for that as much as you obviously did.'

Dan walked over to a log chest beside the fireplace. He opened the lid, drew out a .52 Spencer carbine, and handed it to Curly. 'Listen to Hensa. It'll be up to both of you, if you think it's worth it.'

Cool night air drifted into the ranch house, and Dan shoved the door.

'Ride east, Curly. Will's out there somewhere. He's not far away, and he'll see you. Tell him what's going on. Tell him to make for the border, and then let the sheriff know.'

Dan had waited for Will to get near the border, then rode the five miles to Eagle Spring.

Opposite the River Bend Saloon was a telegraph agency, and Dan sent a message to his commanding officer at West Point.

He led his pony along to the hitching rail outside the sheriff's office where Lummock was working on a reward notice. The sheriff snorted and observed his handiwork. 'Maybe not so good, but good enough.'

'Why do you need a notice if I'm bringing him in? I know what Will looks like, remember.'

Lummock laid the notice aside. He fumbled in the drawer of his desk, and flipped a silver star to his new deputy. 'Your badge of office.'

Dan caught it, and put it in his vest pocket. 'I'll wear it when I'm sworn in. What about Will, and that reward notice?'

Lummock rose heavily from his desk. 'He's on the border, so it's for someone else. You'll be in charge here. There's a little

21

something that needs my personal attention.' Lummock grinned overbearingly at Dan. 'A deputy's just what I needed...' He stopped just short of 'boy'.

A little before noon, he saw the sheriff leave town and head south. The sun was high, and there was little activity around Main Street.

He checked into the small hotel, where he'd been full-boarded. As his meal was set in front of him, he heard a light chuckle from the door. It was Goose Parker, standing there with his daughter, Filena. The Parkers saw Dan and walked towards him. It had been five years since he had last seen Filena. She had gone East to live with her mother and Dan had not heard of her since. She held out her hand, and he took it nervously. From the young and wilful trifler he remembered, she'd grown beautiful. Her eyes were as dark as her hair, and her skin was the colour of an autumn leaf.

'Welcome home, Daniel. What a pleasant coincidence.'

He blushed with surprise, then spoke to her father. But he couldn't take his eyes from Filena, who looked so decorative and proud. Like the scion of an Indian chief. He pulled out another chair. 'Please join me.'

Parker looked at the plate of food on Dan's table. 'No, you finish your meal, Daniel. Perhaps we'll talk later.' Parker started to move away. 'I'm pleased to hear you've taken up the sheriff's offer. We need young men like you. Will you be bringing your brother in to Eagle Spring?'

'It's warranted as murder, so I have to, yes. I'm a law officer.'

'It's a shame you weren't a law officer when it happened,' Filena said.

Before Dan could answer, Parker steered his daughter away. 'I'm sorry. Finish your meal, Daniel. I meant what I said about you being a deputy sheriff.'

Dan didn't understand Goose Parker. He didn't sound like the character he was supposed to be, and it wasn't in his manner. But he understood Filena. She had a brother too.

Daniel spent the afternoon browsing through the sheriff's records. He examined the Wanted notices, stamping his memory with names and faces.

An hour before dusk, he visited the saloon. It wasn't a pay day, and the bar wasn't crowded. A dishevelled character, goaded by a colleague, turned and watched him. Dan recognized the man. He'd been looking at a portrait of him less than twenty minutes ago, and he nearly recalled the name. The man finished his drink, and took two steps forward. He almost made contact, and Dan reeled from his feral odour.

There was no doubt, it was meant to be a rough test of Daniel's character and, as he considered a move, he wondered why Lummock hadn't done anything. The poster had been on his desk. ESCAPED CONVICT. ARMED ROBBERY. DENVER. COLORADO. That was 600 miles west, and the man's name was Joseph 'Joe' Church.

Dan drew his gun, and nudged the long barrel gently into the man's stomach. 'I don't like to interrupt a man's drinking, but now you're finished, and under arrest.'

Church was too amazed to respond. His mouth opened and he stared blank-eyed at the deputy. Dan saw Church's partner reach inside his coat, and he swung the .44 towards the ground. He pulled the trigger and a bullet tore into the man's foot fractionally before the barrel went back into Church's vest. The man was cursing, and howling with pain, but Dan pressed his advantage.

He whispered, close, to the side of Church's face, 'I know what you're thinking, Joe Church from Denver, but it's a single-action Smith & Wesson. You wouldn't have time.'

Dan turned to the few customers of the saloon. 'If any of you good citizens feel a need to help, go get a doctor for that man. This one's going back to Colorado.'

The noise of Dan's gun brought Carver

Hayes from his office. He stared in disbelief.

Dan nodded at him. 'Good evening, Mr Hayes. We seem to be giving your friends a bad time at this bar.'

Hayes saw one of his hired men with a smashed, crimson foot, and another with a gun stuck in his belly. He managed to contain his feelings, and slammed his office door behind him.

Dan relieved the outlaw of his gun, a Le Mat grapeshot, and nudged him into Main Street towards the jail. He kicked the town marshal awake, and told him to unlock a cell.

Church cursed, and Dan pushed him forward. 'Make yourself at home, Joe. There's a pail, but the county don't run to bathing facilities.' Daniel locked the door and turned away. 'It's only the money I'm interested in, nothing personal.'

The town marshal showed a sudden interest. 'The sheriff ain't gunna like this. It'll get him madder'n hell. Yes, sir.'

Dan walked past him and joked, 'It's me

you should be worried about, Jigger. If he gets out, you'll owe me the five-hundred-dollars reward.'

As Daniel returned to the sheriff's office, Jigger flapped his elbows. He peered into the jail, then replaced his chair on the boardwalk. 'Turkey cock. Somebody's gunna make a lead dumplin' with that boy's ass.'

3

Dan Glass Deputy Sheriff

It was several days before the sheriff returned to Eagle Spring. Joseph Church continued to sweat in the jail, cursing and blistering the ears of passers-by. Carver Hayes was waiting to see Dan. He wanted bail for the prisoner.

Dan grinned and shook his head. 'I haven't the authority to set bail, and you know it. That's for the district judge to decide. Church is wanted for robbery and jailbreak, and he's staying where he is. At least until Lummock gets back.'

Hayes recognized the problem. As long as the sheriff was away, the deputy held the cards, and the circuit judge wouldn't fix bail for an escaped convict. Hayes employed

Church to protect his interests in the saloon, as well as his own personal safety, and the man wasn't earning his pay sitting in jail.

Hayes's temper got the better of him. 'Every night someone rides in with a price on his head. It doesn't bother Lummock. He turns a blind eye, as long as they keep their noses clean. There's probably half a dozen in my place right now, and most are from outa state.'

Lummock's wayward law annoyed and provoked Dan. Perhaps it would do the same to Carver Hayes.

Dan took off his hat and pitched it across the office. 'That may be so, but Church stays until Lummock decides to release him.'

When Hayes returned to the saloon, he snatched at a bottle of whiskey, and beckoned two men to his office. If Deputy Glass continued to act as an honest law officer, River Bend would have to watch out. The profits wouldn't be as high.

Back at the sheriff's office, Dan was toying

with the notices of several wanted men. He pushed one into his open vest, slotted his revolver and holster onto his belt, and went out.

When he reached the saloon, he pushed back the swing doors and walked straight to the bar. 'Where's Hayes?' he asked the bartender.

The man was spooning out pickled eggs, and he nodded towards the closed door at the back. 'In his office.' But when Dan started for the door the bartender held up his hand. 'Best wait 'til he comes out, Deputy.'

There was a clear message in his voice, a note of warning. Dan stopped. 'It'll wait then. Just tell him I want to have a word.'

Taking an egg from the barman's dipper, he went outside and stood, back against the saloon wall. A cowboy came out and nodded to him, and Dan watched as he led his horse along Main Street to the livery stable.

Within a few minutes another man

followed. But he didn't see the deputy, until he felt the muzzle of a .44 Smith & Wesson thrust into the base of his spine.

'Judging by the Wanted poster I've got here, you've a rare likeness to Injun McTell. Right down to that painful acne.' Dan lifted the man's coat and gingerly felt around his vest for the Apache pistol.

McTell started to argue, but Dan closed him down with a broad smile.

'We don't need a ruckus. This is between you and me. Get yourself to the jail, and tell Marshal Jigger to put you in a cell. If you don't, I'll come after you and slice your jaw off. Then I'll tie you to your horse and send you into the Breaks.' It was Dan's smile that sent fear through McTell.

Later, when Dan arrived at the jail, McTell was penned up next to Church. Dan told Jigger to take away their buckets if they spoke to each other, 'And if they start crowin' throw the piss over 'em.'

'Pouring piss over prisoners ain't what I'm used to.'

Dan grinned. 'Just think what I've got in mind for you, Jigger, if you don't keep your mouth shut.'

Later the same afternoon, Dan arrested another wanted man. It was the cowboy who had led his horse to the livery stable. He hadn't recognized him at first, only later when he checked the notices. Using the same brand of startling charm, he jailed the cattle thief from Wyoming alongside his partners.

It was mid-evening before Carver Hayes missed his men. No one had seen them, and he was worried.

He'd anticipated something going wrong, and Dan Glass had something to do with it. He couldn't involve Lummock, and didn't need banking advice from Thomas Feigh.

There was a light in the sheriff's office, and Hayes saw Dan slumped at a desk. His eyes were closed, and he held a few reward notices in his hand. Others were strewn across the floor.

Dan blinked as he looked up, but responded courteously as the saloon owner came in.

'Good evening, Mr Hayes. Come to see me?'

Hayes used his gambler's front to disguise his impatience. 'Jack said you wanted to see me.'

'Oh yes.' Dan pushed the notices aside. 'It was to let you know I wasn't favouring Joe Church and his friends.' He squinted hard across the office at Hayes. 'Hardly fair to arrest him, with most of his cronies living it up in your saloon.' Dan's look softened. 'You visited my hoose-gow recently?'

Hayes smirked. 'You've let Church go. I knew you'd see it my way in the end, Deputy.'

Dan stood, and faced Hayes squarely. 'No, you misunderstand. They're *all* there now. Church, McTell, and the rustler from Wyoming. They're tucked up nice and friendly-like, hugger-mugger for market.'

Hayes *had* misunderstood, and was

startled. 'That could be a big mistake, Glass.'

He stormed from the sheriff's office, and went straight for the jail. Jigger hadn't the nerve to stop him, and there were howls of resentment from the prisoners. Hayes took one long hard look, slammed the jail door against the frightened marshal, and returned to the sheriff's office. He was almost on the run, his body quivering with anger.

'You whelp. You've no jurisdiction to lock up those men.

Dan was unmoved. 'Your friends weren't pleased to see you, Mr Hayes? They're all wanted somewhere, but it's for the sheriff to decide where. Meanwhile they stay in jail.'

Before dawn, news would reach the nearby ranches. Regardless of jurisdiction, the new deputy had jailed three law-breakers.

Sheriff Lummock rode back into town the next morning. When he saw the prisoners he almost had a seizure. 'You young fool,' he exploded. 'What in hell's name do you think you're doing? They're not wanted in Stover County. They've broke no law in this town. Turn 'em out.'

Dan had intentionally bent the law. But to innocent, law-abiding people, outlaws were being released into their town.

The ranch was coming up for auction, and Dan made several trips back to Horse Creek to see Hensa and Curly. The Piney, and its water, still belonged to the Glass spread, but if the town 'cartel' became its new owners, they would have a stranglehold on the smaller ranchers.

Curly had become accomplished with the carbine and its measure. There had been no word from Will, but it didn't concern Dan. The deputy knew his brother was capable of looking out for himself.

On the day of the auction, two men climbed from a tilbury wagon. Not many would have recognized Hensa's partner as the dishevelled and reclusive Curly, with his white vest, tie and stick-pin. His feet were squeezed into shiny black boots, and he carried the big Spencer carbine. Main street was grouped with stock wagons and horses, and there was an open Conestoga in from Newburg.

Hensa tied their wagon to the hitching rail in front of the hotel, and Curly picked up a money draft on a Missouri bank. Genuine friendship and acceptance meant more to Curly than any amount of money. After ten years, he'd found a worthy and deserving use for it.

Dan found them out back of the hotel where the auction was to be held. He looked serious when he saw Hensa with a Navy Colt tucked into the band of his pants, but grinned when he saw Curly's suit. 'You look smart, Curly. Someone's going to get a big surprise when you buy the Horse Creek.'

They'd been standing at the rear of the hotel for a while when Curly whispered,

'Will's coming into town. I told him to stay away, but he wants to see the auction run legal, and I think he wants to see you, Dan.'

Sheriff Lummock stepped onto a makeshift platform, and Thomas Feigh stood close for any financial, or legal phrasing. Among the crowd, Dan saw Carver Hayes, with Joe Church lingering in the background.

Lummock read out a description of the property, and the request to bid got started. A man at the back opened with a desultory offer, and Dan turned to look. Feigh and the 'cartel' were obviously teasing for a serious buyer, but eventually the banker gave Hayes his signal for the 'shock' bid. It was Curly, though, who raised the bid before Goose Parker stepped in. Both bids were unexpected, and Dan saw the banker's startled expression. He looked to Parker, but it was beyond that he glimpsed the fleeting figure of his brother. Eagle Spring was the last place he wanted to see Will, as long as he was deputy sheriff. He hoped that

Curly, or Lummock, hadn't caught sight of him.

Dan switched his attention back to Thomas Feigh. There was something wrong. Goose Parker was bidding against Feigh and Hayes. But why? Just as it looked as though the ranch was going to Parker, Curly yelled, 'Five thousand.'

A murmur of surprise, disbelief, then approval came from a few people in the hotel. Mostly they didn't know Curly Boyd, had never really wanted to. But they knew he was a friend of the Glass family, and because of the headwater, a more agreeable, and co-operative owner of the ranch.

Feigh's face had turned sickly grey. He'd prompted Hayes to raise bids, but the saloon owner failed to react. It was clear he couldn't move any higher. As auctioneer, Sheriff Lummock had no choice but to knock the ranch down to Curly.

At the courthouse, Curly tendered the money draft, and had the Horse Creek deed recorded. Dan told Curly to follow on and, with Hensa, led a small, cheerful crowd to the saloon. Dan suddenly remembered Will, and looked cautiously around, but he'd vanished.

Dan was reaching to the swing doors of the saloon, when somebody crashed into the path of Hensa. It was Joseph 'Joe' Church, and he wasn't as drunk as he made out.

Dan stepped back, shook his head, and groaned, 'Oh no.'

Church leered at Hensa. 'You know this boy sheriff? The lock-up kid?' Without warning, he whirled, and pushed his hand into Dan's face. His hand reached for the Le Mat he carried strapped around his chest, but even before he drew the gun, Hensa had his Colt levelled at the back of Church's head.

A break in the walkway had momentarily tripped Dan, and he was off balance. All he saw was the grapeshot revolver and a heavy thumb easing the hammer. He was wondering about his next move, and the time he had left, when from the other side of the street, two shots crashed out in quick succession.

Church lifted himself onto his toes as the first bullet tore into his chest. Then he snapped forward as the second took him at waist level, destroying his gun and his hand at the same time. His face was gripped with astonishment as he stared down at fingers that were jellied to his gun. With one hand he reached out for Dan, closed his eyes, and fell to the street.

Lummock came running from the hotel clutching a rifle, stopping short as he saw Church's lifeless form ahead of him. He saw Deputy Glass picking himself from the street and rubbing his shoulder. For a moment, the sheriff couldn't understand what had happened. He'd expected to see the deputy lying lifeless in the street. He looked round and saw Curly approaching from the courthouse, his carbine still in its scabbard. Hensa was standing calm and pokerfaced, his Colt unused.

From across the street Will sat calmly on

his pony. His Smith & Wesson was pointing straight at Lummock. 'Who's to do your killing now, Sheriff?'

There was no other sound, just Will's voice, and a yapping mongrel. 'Next time I'll come for *you*, Lummock. Go talk to Carver about a loser's streak.' He turned and looked at the small crowd of onlookers. 'There's an election not far away. You know who'll do you a good job. You people oughta get smart.'

Will gently spurred the pony, and cantered up Main Street. He headed out of town, west, towards the foothills of the Ozarks.

Hensa and Curly had boarded the wagon and, from the street, Dan slapped at the dusty flanks of their plod mare.

In the middle of the street, one of the ranchers who'd suffered from the town cartel turned solemnly to his wife. 'I'm going for a drink with Tommy Dinner and Zeke. There's talk of a new sheriff.'

4

Cotton Parker Comes to Eagle Spring

The men ambled toward the River Bend Saloon, but stopped when Carver Hayes suddenly appeared. One of his henchmen was lying dead in the street, and Lummock was staring bewildered at the lifeless body.

The saloon owner swore, looked at Dan, then spoke sharply to Lummock. 'You'd better get Glass to a safe place before the boys see this.'

It was too much for Curly. He swung the tip of the Spencer to the underside of Hayes's jaw. He pressed it hard against bone, and stared into the man's face. 'You're the one that needs a safe place, Mr Hayes. And if I could prove you were...'

Curly's emotional exchange trailed off, and Hayes shook himself free. 'I was talking to the sheriff, you miserable–'

Hensa edged a shoulder into the small space between Hayes and Curly. 'Stay out, Curly. He don't know how this happened. He guesses.'

Then Dan shook his head, and laid his hand on Curly's arm. 'He's no idea who killed him.'

'Who killed him, Glass?' Hayes asked Dan.

Lummock roused himself from his thoughts, and interrupted. 'It was his brother.'

For the sheriff, it suddenly didn't look that good. Possibly he saw himself in Joe Church. He seemed dazed by the killing at his feet, and spoke to himself more than anyone else. 'He was defending Dan. He'd done no wrong; we all saw. Somebody get the body moved.'

Dan waited until the coffin-maker had removed Church's body, then met Curly and Hensa at the bar.

Tommy Dinner met them, smiling and effusive. 'We been talkin' it over, Dan. What this county needs is a new sheriff. Would you accept, if we nominated, and supported you?'

Will had clearly made them all think fast, and if Dinner and a few more of the ranchers were prepared to back him, it was an idea. But he had the immediate dilemma of acting out his role as deputy. When Lummock had collected himself, he'd probably organize a posse for Will.

Dan nodded. 'Only if there's enough backing, Tom. Then I'll be glad to at least stand.'

The old rancher shook Dan's hand. 'Well done, well done.'

Ezekiel Box suggested another round of drinks, but the bartender looked doubtfully at Hayes. He was talking to Sheriff Lummock and Goose Parker's son, Cotton. The saloon owner told the barman to give them a round on the house.

On the way back to the hotel, with Dan and Curly, Hensa looked uneasy. 'They'll fight nasty. You'll be up against four.'

Dan smiled kindly at his old friend. 'Yeah, I know.'

As they entered the hotel, the bell above the door jangled. One or two of the customers looked up, and Curly nudged Dan in the side. 'Who's that Dan? Not the Parker girl, is it?'

After their meal, Goose Parker spoke to Dan about the job of sheriff. He introduced Curly and Hensa to Filena, then kept Dan talking for ten minutes. Dan wanted to speak to Filena, but when he went outside, Curly had already volunteered to take her home. Dan laughed quietly into the evening sky as Filena and Curly climbed into the tilbury wagon. He watched as they swung round towards Goose Pond, and didn't notice the man who slipped out of the darkness into the River Bend Saloon.

Dan went back into the hotel, and nodded at Hensa who appeared half asleep. His hat was tilted down on his forehead, but the look was deceptive. Now that Dan had agreed to stand as sheriff, he was wakeful and cautious.

Dan sat and talked events with Goose Parker, then later he met several other ranchers, and they discussed the possible withdrawal of water rights. They sat outside and, although it was dark, there was enough moonlight for Dan to make out the figure of Thomas Feigh entering the bank. A few minutes later, Hayes and Lummock followed. The cartel had decided to call a short-notice meeting, and Dan was tempted to listen in. He made excuses about night watch, and wandered off towards the sheriff's office. He then doubled back, and approached the bank in the off-street darkness. He pulled off his boots, and climbed to the roof. Walking carefully, he reached a skylight directly over Feigh's office, through the dust of which he could just make out figures of three men. Within moments there was a sharp rap from below him, and Dan instinctively shrank back. Lummock got up, opened the door, and Cotton Parker swaggered in. He was obviously drunk, and he belched loudly, as he sat at Feigh's table. The voices were blurred, and Dan could only catch a word here and there, but he sensed they were talking about him.

He heard Carver Hayes say, 'How about that other matter?'

The banker was shaking his head. 'Nothing definite. But it's still our blue chip. I've written to the Department of the Interior.'

A short, heated argument followed, in which Cotton Parker seemed to join in. The men had a problem, but after a while, they all got up and left Feigh's office. Dan lay still for a few minutes, then made his way down. He grabbed at his boots, and walked thoughtfully towards the sheriff's office. Now he knew. Goose Parker wasn't connected with the men who were squeezing the town, it was Cotton. The increase in

Goose Pond stock, was probably due to breeding, not rustling.

An unsteady voice called his name, and he stopped and waited as the man weaved towards him. The glow from a streetside window lit up the side of the man's face. Dan wasn't surprised to be confronted by Cotton Parker.

'Hello Cotton. What can the deputy sheriff do for you?'

Parker stopped in the street, a few feet from Dan. He moved his feet apart to give himself more stability, and swayed gently from the hips. It was the classic stance of a drunk who wanted a fight.

'The deputy can stay away from my sister. And then stay away from me, and everyone ... you'll be sorry if you don't ... I'll be here in the morning ... will you?'

Dan was worried about what Cotton Parker was trying to say. 'What do you think's going to happen to me, Cotton?'

Parker seemed to realize that he'd said too much, and tried something more personal.

'Come on, Dan. Don't need anyone to do it for me, do I? Come on, try me.'

Dan stared down at Parker. For a long time there'd been friction. They were roughly the same age, but as youngsters, Cotton had always been bigger, and had the muscle that went with it. Will had often rescued Dan after a roughing-up.

Dan looked around him, but the street was dark and deserted. He stepped off the boardwalk, and Parker smiled as he started to undo his gunbelt. But it was a cheat for what he did next. His right hand swung up, aiming for the beak of Dan's face. Dan sensed the movement and side-stepped with a fast punch. It was vicious, and cracked Parker's nose, spurting bright, thin blood. Parker's face quivered close to Dan, as he attempted to focus. He wanted something to strike back at. It was mindless coming in again, and Dan stood his ground, watching the reckless swing. The fist was easy to dodge, and Dan stepped inside making a hard, low stab into the side of Parker's head.

Parker fell to his knees, slobbering, as Dan stood over him. He unwound himself into a crouch, while Dan took his time, aiming coldly with his toe. It was getting late, and the day was over for Cotton Parker. The fray ended as suddenly as it begun, and Parker was in no condition to take any more. Dan wiped his hands across the front of his vest, and then lumped Parker across to the jail. Jigger was snoring peacefully on a cot, and Dan knee'd him in the side.

'It's me again, Jigger. Where's the keys? There's a drunk here, needs cooling off. Turn him out when he sobers up.'

The marshal looked at the battered face of Cotton Parker, then at Dan. 'I recognize something there, don't I? Underneath the blood.'

'Yeah. It's a good job I'm resigning as deputy. I could charge him with resisting arrest or something.'

Jigger had his usual look of worry and burden. 'You're really tuggin' on Lummock's rope. Those two are closer'n snake's

51

belly and sand.'

Dan looked a little more understanding. 'OK, Jigger. If you're that concerned, do what you like with him. It's late and I'm going to the hotel.'

The marshal lost no time in trying to bring Parker round. He doused him with water, and dabbed at his wounds with a bandanna. He tipped some coffee through his broken lips, and then walked him around the cell. He found Parker's horse and brought it round to the rear of the jail. He was interested to hear what had happened, but Parker scowled, and told him to get out of the way. Jigger slapped the horse tamely, and watched it canter off to Goose Pond.

Two miles out of town, Parker met Curly in the tilbury wagon, heading east to Horse Creek.

'I just been to your place,' Curly shouted. Then as he got close, he saw Parker's face, doughy and ashen in the moonlight. 'Jeez, what happened to you? Meet someone from the past?'

Parker spat a hurtful insult at Curly. But he'd already come off second best, and noticed the Spencer, resting between Curly's boots.

Curly shrugged and flicked the reins. 'Look's like Dan been doin' more of that deputy sheriff work, Brownie.' He giggled, and the mule's ears twitched.

As Parker pounded off in the direction of his father's ranch, Curly spoke again to the mule. 'I've made a decision. I haven't got time for commitment, and so I'm leaving Miss Parker for Dan. She'll take it hard, but it's for the best.' He kicked the footboard and called into the night, 'Let's go home.'

5

Back from the Dead

On his way back to the hotel, Dan went to the sheriff's office. There was a lamp still lit, but Lummock wasn't there. He sat at the desk, and thoughtfully penned his resignation. The way it stood, he'd had enough of being a deputy. Several times he glanced at the clock, but guessed the sheriff was drowning his troubles.

Cotton Parker's words had given Dan something to think about. There was no doubt in his mind they'd already tried to kill him. That was Joe Church. And there was no doubt they'd try again. But it would be different next time. It would be a bullet out of the darkness, or a knife in an alleyway. He thought back to the snatch of conversation he'd overheard from the bank. What had Feigh meant, by saying that he'd written to the Department of the Interior?

Cotton Parker didn't strike Dan as a killer. Nevertheless, there were two bullets in the old man, and long distance with a rifle didn't require the same nerve as face to face. And, how much did Goose Parker know about his own son?

It was getting late, but Dan's mind wandered on. He couldn't understand how any profit from Goose Pond helped the cartel. Thomas Feigh's interest was a deed-mortgage on practically every ranch in the county, with the exception of Goose Pond. What Sheriff Lummock stood to gain was less obvious, although with Feigh as a land and cattle baron, he'd have powerful support. Carver Hayes's profit would come from a wide-open gambling empire.

Then another thought came to him: what would they do about Curly? Try and destroy him? That wouldn't get them Horse Creek, or water rights of the Piney. Besides, it would probably bring in a United States marshal.

Deciding it was useless to wait for the sheriff, Dan locked the door and walked to the hotel. But this time he did notice someone moving in the shadows.

In his room, Dan calmly lit a lamp. He pushed up the window, and pulled down the roller blind. He took two pillows, and pressed them roughly into the shape of a sleeping body and placed them on the bed. Then he covered them with a blanket. He put his hat on the bedside chair and placed his belt and holster on the pillow, close to where his head should have been. He spread a few of his other clothes around the room, turned out the lamp, and pulled the blind back open. Standing back from the moonlight that filtered into the room, Dan peered into the alleys that fronted main street. There was nothing moving, just muffled noise from the River Bend Saloon.

After an hour watching, he drew a blanket around his shoulders and crouched in the corner to one side of the window. In the moonlight, the pillows made a convincing silhouette of a man sleeping.

Dan snoozed for almost an hour, then twitched at the sound of scraping along the window ledge. The moon was lower, and from the window the shape on the bed was clearly outlined. He gripped the .44 Smith & Wesson, and held very still. A hand appeared across the ledge, followed almost instantly, and silently, by the head and shoulders of a dark figure. For a moment the man listened, the thin light outlining his long hair and battered sombrero. Dan saw the gleam on the steel of a knife, and he watched, breathless, as the man's arm swung in a fast, sideways arc. The air stilled, then thudded, as the knife flashed into the curved lump across the bed. Then Dan moved. He unwound from his crouched position and slammed the frame of his gun into the side of his assailant's head. As the man fell, Dan gripped his wrist, and swung him to the side of the bed. He used the lanyard of the man's skinning knife to bind his wrists, and his own belt to wrap around his ankles. Dan had a quick look across the street, levered the man out onto the narrow, wooden sill, and rolled him into a rough fall. He wouldn't die, but there might be a broken bone or two. Dan dropped to the ground a few seconds later. He heard the soft snuffle of a horse from somewhere across the street, and he half dragged, half carried the man towards the sound. Dan hoped it was the man's horse, as he pushed the body up behind the saddle.

He headed the horse out to Horse Creek. The animal was good, and struck a medium pace. They crossed the dried bed of the Piney and dipped towards the ranch house. He drew rein outside the cabin, and yelled for some attention.

Curly came hustling through the door in a night shirt, brandishing Hensa's Navy Colt. 'What in hell's name...?'

Dan laughed. 'You look cute in fancy dress, Curly. Help me get this down, will you?'

Hensa watched from a side window as Dan and Curly dragged the body into the house.

Curly stared at the man on the floor, then looked inquisitively at Dan. 'I saw Cotton Parker not long ago. Looked to me like someone got real mad with his face.' He turned back to the man on the floor who was beginning to raise himself onto an elbow. 'And who the hell's this?'

Dan stepped up close. 'This, my friend, is the man who thought he'd knifed the deputy sheriff to death.'

The man dragged himself to a semi-crouched position and spoke to Dan's boots. 'Who are you?'

Dan kicked the man's hands out from under him. 'Me? You ugly son of a bitch, *I'm* the deputy sheriff.'

Curly knelt close to the man, and untied his wrists. 'Tell us your name, mister.'

The man kept his mouth closed. He was trying to figure out where he was, and what had happened to him. He looked up at Dan.

'Who'd you say you were?'

'As far as you're concerned, Deputy Sheriff Dan Glass. You knifed two pillows at the hotel. Now who are you? And who paid you to kill me?'

The man looked insolently at Curly, then Hensa.

Daniel leant down and untied his belt from around the man's boots. Then, without warning, he lashed it across the man's eyes. He blazed with anger. 'You tried to kill me, scum-sucker! Now tell us.'

The man groaned with hurt, and clutched his face. He spat at Dan's feet, and tried to raise himself.

Dan could see he wasn't going to give, and spoke flatly. 'Suit yourself. Lummock and Hayes'll already have a search party out. They're not going to want you around.'

The man scowled, and swayed sideways. He still couldn't understand the predicament he was in. 'You say you're the deputy sheriff?' Something was edging into his brain, but there was nothing coming out.

Dan smiled almost kindly at the man. 'Goodbye, mister. Curly, tie his hands again, then hang him in the barn.'

Hensa turned, and walked up to Curly. 'I'll help.'

The man still seemed indifferent to his fate as Hensa prodded him outside. Curly held an oil lamp, and the three of them walked down to the barn. Hensa stopped, then looked hard at the man.

'Sometimes Dan Glass gets very angry. People trying to kill him all the time. You stay here for a while.' He kicked the man's feet from under him, and he fell heavily into the open corn crib.

Curly wedged a stave across the long topflap, and banged it tight with his fist. 'And keep quiet, or I'll get the rope.'

Dan told Curly he was getting his head down for a couple of hours. 'There's some faces I want to see in the morning, just after they've seen mine. All the better since they won't be able to find that pig you didn't hang.' He looked coyly at the new owner of his ranch. 'How did you make out with Filena?'

Curly enjoyed the amicable rib, and caught the expression in Dan's eyes. 'She's all fleece, and a mile wide. Yes sir, we hit it off like a couple of doves. By the way, what was it you said you overheard, about the Interior Department? That's in Washington, isn't it?'

Dan shrugged. 'That was it, all of it. Department of the Interior. That's all I heard.'

'Talk to Zeke Box, then. He knows someone in Washington, doesn't he? I hope something happens around here soon that involves me.'

'Keep your powder dry, Curly. There'll be action soon enough, without you hoping for it.'

Back at Eagle Spring, in the River Bend Saloon, Lummock and Hayes were opening another bottle. Finch, the 'breed, had brought them good news. They were celebrating the death of the deputy sheriff.

Carver Hayes didn't give orders then blithely expect them to be carried out; he sent a man to watch another man. Finch had remained out of sight, further down the alleyway, until he'd heard the hooves of the knifeman's horse. He'd quickly climbed the front of the hotel and looked into the small room – to be fooled by a likeness, a knife deep in its side.

'We're looking to your re-election, Sheriff.' Hayes poured himself another drink, and Lummock looked smug.

Hayes looked appreciatively at his whiskey. 'How are we going to handle Feigh?'

Lummock was a little confused. 'Well, we took care of Glass.'

'Yes, Sheriff. I just wanted to know you're still with us. We'll sort out the banker when we have to.'

In the meantime, Dan had left Horse Creek. At three in the morning, he had no difficulty in reaching the town unseen. He left the horse in the alley where he'd found it, climbed through the window to his room and cleared the bed. He lay there staring at the ceiling.

With his eyes still bleary from the whiskey, the sheriff walked into his office. It was late in the morning, but Dan was in the wash-house, waiting. The sheriff slumped at his desk, and the first thing that caught his eye was Dan's resignation. It struck him funny, and he sniggered.

'What's the joke, Lummock?' Dan's voice made the sheriff roll in his chair. Lummock's eyes bulged, and it took him a while to focus properly. He wanted the privy, but his legs refused to move. His hands were trembling, and sweat beaded across his forehead.

The sheriff's disposition made it certain. Someone had told him Dan was dead. Lummock raised his eyes, and felt his life hanging by a thin thread.

Dan took a step towards him and the

sheriff recoiled. Dan curled his fingers around the butt of his gun, and Lummock's face turned sickly as he found his voice. He croaked, 'What do you want?' Saliva flecked into the corners of his mouth. 'I didn't try to kill you.'

Dan laughed, but his face was grim. 'What're you talking about now, Sheriff?'

The sheriff looked bewildered, and his mood became crafty., 'I was laughing at your resignation. That's what we were celebrating. That doesn't surprise you, does it?'

'You didn't know about my resignation then, Lummock. You were celebrating me being dead.' Dan stepped nearer the desk, deciding to bluff the sheriff. 'I'm not going to kill you, Lummock. Although you tried to get me killed yesterday, and then again, last night. I want you to think on this: Joe Church didn't die in the street, he died in his coffin.'

Lummock's face sagged, and he looked resigned and vague.

Dan pushed his face in close. 'You need a lot to get out of this. Church spoke to me before he died. It wasn't his confession, but he gave me enough. The judge should have it by now.'

A little of the sheriff's courage seemed to return, and he came blustering to his feet.

Dan quickly pulled Lummock's gun from its holster, and poked it into the big man's stomach. 'Steady, Sheriff. Something happening to me would be the fastest way to get a US marshal here.' He turned the Colt in his hand, and placed it on the desk. 'You don't need this, do you, *boy*?'

Lummock sat down again. He couldn't think what Church might have said. It was just the uncertainty. Someone like Church probably used information as insurance.

For a long time after Dan had gone, Lummock thought on the warning. He decided it required a better head than his, and he almost ran to the banker's office. Thomas Feigh was no killer gunman, but he was the most cold-blooded of the group. His world was money and power, and he considered himself the brains of the cartel. Carver Hayes was priced down as inferior, and Lummock an oaf of limited use. As for Cotton Parker, he was a braggadocio, and becoming tiresome and difficult.

The banker had to make plans and, after hearing the sheriff's story, he set up a meeting of the cartel in the early afternoon.

6

Curly Takes a Hand

Dan gave up his role as deputy sheriff, and returned to Horse Creek. Except for the occasional loss of a heifer, it had been a reasonable year on the ranch. But it wasn't the same for the smaller ranchers to the south and east. Curly allowed their cattle to graze and water on Creek land, but Thomas Feigh had pressed hard. Every further loan had clauses designed to wipe them out.

Unnoticed by the sheriff, Will came back to help Dan, and with Curly, they rode the Breaks, figuring out a way to defeat their opponents. They were surprised at Curly's horsemanship, and now he'd taken up the gun.

They were leading their ponies through

the foothills, when Curly suddenly stopped. He pulled the Spencer from its scabbard, and sat loose in the saddle. He levered a round into the chamber, and looked hard ahead.

Dan wondered how Curly was going to fire the big carbine and knew it wouldn't be the conventional way. He was right. Curly held the stock tight to his thigh, and pulled the trigger. He levered shells in and out of the gun faster than the brothers thought possible. Curly pounded bullets into a stand pine until it crashed into the canyon thirty yards ahead.

He looked coolly at Will and Dan. 'Hensa showed me. And if you think that was good, you should see *him*.'

When they reached the grazing ground, back near Horse Creek, Curly said, 'I'm still learning about cattle, but it seems we could do with new stock to upgrade.'

Will looked surprised. 'Yes, you're right, Curly. You could go to the bank and speak to Feigh. He should know the market.'

The following day Curly went to see Thomas Feigh, and the banker told him of some stock near the border country, 500 cross-bred shorthorns.

Within a few days, the men rode out to inspect the herd. They couldn't find anything wrong with the animals, or the sale. The brands had been run over, but that was usual with border mavericks. Dan hired a drover to help with the drive, and they headed back to Horse Creek.

There was no sign of trouble until the cattle were in the dry, lower reaches of the Piney. They'd camped for the night near the outlying borders of the ranch. Come daybreak, the drover was missing.

'That's mighty odd,' Curly said. 'He didn't even stay to get paid.'

'Don't worry about it,' Will said. 'We can handle the drive from now on. Let's move, I'm tired of sowbelly an' beans.'

Once the animals were up and moving, Dan took point. They rode in trio outside the cattle, and Will and Curly took turns dropping back to pick up scatterlings. The ground was packed hard, but the surface billowed thick around them. They were completely hidden from each other, and they drew bandannas tight around their faces.

They heard the Spencer carbine as its crash rebounded across the low foothills. Will came at the gallop, and Dan swung away from the point.

They found Curly crowding a group of cattle drovers. One of them was clutching his lower leg trying to staunch the flow of blood. Curly 'heehawed', and turned to face Dan and Will.

'These men believe our herd's stolen. Him, riding the grey, was thinking to use his rifle. He's lucky not to have *lost* his leg.'

Will looked across the group. 'Who are you men?'

A man without a hat, or hair, said, 'I'm the ramrod of the Bent Horn. And our brand's on most of them cows.'

Will looked over the herd and nodded.

'Hmm. That's a possibility, mister. But we've got a bill of sale, and you should see what Curly's gun does from *close* range.'

The ramrod ran his hand across the top of his head and looked at the sweat on his fingers. 'Maybe you got a bill of sale, and maybe you haven't. It doesn't matter to me. Every ranch in the county is losing stock. Most of them are driven straight to the border where you picked those up.'

Will said, almost friendly-like, 'This is getting us nowhere. We paid a good price for the cattle, and we're not handing them over to you, or anyone else. Now it seems to me, ramrod, that you could improve your health by riding on. We'll be at Horse Creek if anyone has a complaint to make.'

The ramrod looked hard at the brothers. He saw the stone resolve, and wasn't going up against it. He pulled up his horse's head, and looked at Will. 'I'll see you around. I know who you are.'

Will shook his head and smiled. 'Yeah, well, I feel a lot happier not knowing who the hell you are.'

As the men from the Bent Horn rode off, Dan spun towards Curly. 'Of *course*. When you went to see Thomas Feigh. He saw the move. He organized a make-up herd to be run to the border. They all knew I'd go to help with the drive. Daniel Glass, the prospective sheriff, with five hundred recently stolen cross-bred shorthorns. Neat, eh?'

Will looked at his brother seriously. 'Well, we got the bill of sale, and that's good enough for me. That's why the drover took off. He was told to.' He smiled and looked at Curly. 'You had the use of a drover for nothing, boss.'

Curly went thoughtful. The cattle were bought out of state. He'd paid honest money, and everyone knew you picked up bad steers in a bundle. But as a defence it didn't amount to a hill of beans.

The sun was a low golden shimmer when the cattle drifted into the Horse Creek herd. The weary cowboys dismounted at the corral, where Walt, the ranch hand, waited for news. He pushed back his worn Stetson and squinted at Dan.

'There was a stranger came looking for you. I saw no reason to lie. Sounds like there's going to be trouble.'

To Will's great satisfaction, Walt dished up steak, with eggs and potatoes, and no one spoke until they'd finished. He pushed his chair back from the table. 'This doesn't help your election, Dan. It was set-up by Feigh. The news'll travel, and it won't improve in the telling. You could lose a lot of votes.'

Curly looked from Will to Dan. 'We'll hand the cattle over to anyone proving ownership.'

Dan snorted. 'Like hell we will. Is that the best you can come up with, Curly? Those cattle are bought and paid for. Feigh can whistle for 'em.'

'You think maybe they're gonna try and take 'em?' Curly's voice turned hopeful.

Will chuckled. 'Listen to him. Gun-fighting's gone to his head.' He got up and moved towards the rear door. 'I'm going to take me a room in the hay loft. They'll bring Lummock with them. He knows I'm here now.'

Will strolled out to the corral. He pulled his saddle from the rail, and Walt led off the pony. He climbed to the loft, and lay between grain sacks in the open portal.

Dan and Curly took seats on the porch. Curly had his carbine, and Dan held a Winchester across his lap. Walt sat on a bench in front of the bunkhouse, and Hensa sat inside the house. He was facing the door with his Navy Colt balanced on the arm of his chair.

The waiting was broken by the soft rumbling of hooves, west from the low bluffs. Dan and Curly flexed their fingers, and Will stared out from the barn. He called down to Walt who picked up his shotgun and held it across his knees.

When the group of riders emerged from the sunset, Dan counted six, Lummock at the head, and a stranger riding on the flank. With a lot of snorting and creaking of leather, the posse reined up to the ranch house. Lummock eased himself to the ground, then strode up to the two men on the veranda. 'Daniel. Curly.'

Curly said nothing. Dan spoke calmly. 'Sheriff. Nice evening for a ride.' He looked and nodded towards the stranger. 'Or for showing the new deputy how you peace the county?'

The sheriff grinned. 'A bit of both, Dan. I'm following up a report that there's Bent Horn cattle out here. I'm going to look over the herd you just brought in. 'Course I know different. Tom Feigh told me about Curly's buying them.'

Two men drew off from the group, dismounted, and walked towards the corral. One of the two, the bald ramrod of the Bent Horn, turned and looked back at Dan. 'If there's stolen cattle, why not stolen horses?'

Curly looked at Dan, then at the ramrod. 'What else you lookin' for, egg man?'

'Will Glass maybe.' He leered threateningly at Curly.

As a steadying gesture, Dan touched the tip of his rifle against Curly's big carbine. 'This isn't your property, mister, but you're welcome to look. If you've a notion for anything more, forget it.'

The ramrod swore and made a move for his gun. But his hand had only moved a few inches when a rifle shot cracked the air. Dirt spat from between the man's boots, and a wisp of smoke drifted from the grain-gate of the barn.

The sheriff hissed at the ramrod, 'You stupid ... you want to die over some cows? Boyd, show me the sale docket.'

Curly pulled out the crumpled paper. The sheriff read it, and shook his head at the ramrod. 'Looks legitimate. He's a good claim on the herd. We came here looking for stolen cattle, and we haven't found any.

The ramrod of the Bent Horn turned on Dan and Curly. Dan appeared unmoved at his railing, but not Curly. 'This is my land, and my ranch. Get out. Get off my property.'

The ramrod was paying no heed. He spraddled his legs and sneered at Curly. 'If you weren't holding that carbine ... you dumb cripple.'

A fleeting smile flashed across Curly's face, and he let go of the gun. 'How you leaving my ranch? Head up or down?'

The man's eyes flicked with fury, and he drove in with his fists flailing. Curly lashed out at the man's head with a chopping drive, and broke him like a firelog. Before the man could respond, and almost in panic, Curly smashed his bunched fist down on the back of the egg man's neck. He trailed egg man, as he humped along on all fours, pounding short, chopping blows into the man's heavy shoulders. Egg man tried to draw his knees up, but failed, and collapsed into the ground as another blow took him full and low in the back. Curly stood back with his fists still clenched. He knew there was nothing more to do. He was distraught, and his breath came heavy. 'You were told to forget it, egg man.'

Dan and Walt picked up the ramrod, and threw him across his saddle. Dan looked intensely at Lummock. 'I think you'd better leave, Sheriff.'

Lummock looked impressed, and acknowledged Curly. 'That was a fair argument. You've interesting ways about you.'

He glanced once at the barn, as the posse rode away.

7

Bent Horn Takes on Horse Creek

Leading a plough mule, Dan rode to the foothills. He was uneasy about their captive in the line shack. Curly and Hensa had transferred him from the corn crib.

He opened up, and eyed the man coldly. 'We're in for a big rain. The water comes through here waist high.'

The man was still grinding for a fight, but the isolation had worn at his nerves. He looked uneasily at Dan. 'You gonna leave me here?'

'That's up to you. I still want to know who paid you to kill me. A name, and you're free. Or you can rot here. I'll see no one comes through for a month.'

As the door swung closed against him, the

man saw the sky above the distant Ozarks. 'Let me go, and I'll talk.'

With Philun Pegg, the knife-man riding ahead of him, Dan trailed back to the ranch house. Then, an hour later, Curly was standing on the bluff, watching, as Pegg rode out to the county border.

Judge Northwood read the confession that Dan had got from the hired killer. He advised a quick prosecution. 'The county has stood for this for too long.'

Dan was uncertain. 'There're three other men who are just as guilty as Carver Hayes. If he's arrested, we'll prejudice ourselves. Sheriff Lummock'll be on the rampage trying to find Pegg, or his body. They're all worried. Can't you keep this quiet until we get to the others?'

'It would be foolish to wait, Dan,' the judge warned. 'That story about your rustling has spread through the county. There are some knows the truth, but it hasn't helped your campaign.'

But Dan wasn't as keen to win votes as he was to withhold Pegg's evidence against Hayes. He was that determined the judge agreed to hold the signed statement.

The next day, Dan began to work at his campaign. He rode to neighbouring ranches, explaining what he could and *would* do as sheriff.

His travels took him to Goose Pond. Filena was mannerly and cool, and her father met him with a warning. 'The town pack, the "company of wolves" are fixing to dine on your meat, son.' He smiled thinly, depressed, as Dan took a seat on the porch.

'I know that Mr Parker, but I can look after myself.'

Parker nodded gravely, then in what seemed a tactful gesture, he left the room. Dan turned to Filena.

'I'm sorry about that fight I had with your brother. He must have told you, I was only defending myself.'

She looked directly at him. 'I think it

would be much better for all of us, if you took the trouble not to come here again.'

Filena didn't know if that would hurt, and he had no intention of letting her know if it did. There was still hard bark in the Glass family.

'You *do* understand,' she said.

'Yes, I think so. Must be real difficult having Cotton as a brother.'

'What's that to do with it? What do you mean?'

'When I can prove it, Filena, there'll be four men standing trial for the murder of my father. You've thought about it, surely. *You* must know who I'm talking about, but I don't think your father does. Those at the top want Horse Creek, and the headwaters. Surely you know that?'

A shadow cut across Filena as she moved away. 'I'll tell my father you had to go. Please don't come again.'

Dan thrust his feelings away, and swung onto his pony. Without looking back, he spurred deep and headed for Horse Creek.

As he approached the ranch buildings, he heard the distant echo of gunfire from the west. He made a pithy oath, then, levering shells into his Winchester, rode fast towards the sound of gunfire.

The foreman of the Bent Horn had come to collect his cattle.

As Dan topped a low rise, he saw a column of dust. The gunfire had died out, but he could hear the bellowing of the cattle, and the rumble of their hooves. He wasn't close enough to identify the outriders, but they weren't from Horse Creek. One of them wheeled his horse, and came towards him at a dead run. He pulled the Winchester and fired off a quick shot. It raised dust, but the rider came on. He levered another cartridge and aimed. This time the horse dropped to its knees, but the rider jumped clear. He fired once at Dan, then dashed after his companions who were already into the valley.

Two riders came galloping back to cover. They skidded to bale up the man between horses, then raced back to the rear of the herd. With the exception of a few stragglers, the cattle had run into the neck of a valley. Dan rode on, but couldn't see or understand why there was no sign of Curly, Hensa or Walt. And where was his brother? Single-handed he couldn't go up against the men ahead of him.

A rifle bullet whined close to his shoulder, and he fell to the neck of his pony. Grabbing the reins, he rolled from his saddle into the cover of a low cholla.

Dan was wondering about his next move, when out of the valley a sudden burst of gunfire was followed by more bellowing, and screaming from riders. A wedged mass of cattle was struggling to turn in the valley, and from the wild look of the animals, Dan knew the leaders were being pressed hard by those behind.

The crashing of the guns became louder, and he saw three riders in the midst of the herd. They were trapped in a wild cauldron of hoof and horn, madly trying to stay saddled. One trip or stumble would mean terrible injury or death. The riders were firing back over the top of the herd.

Then Dan saw Will and Curly. They'd turned the herd back into the rustlers, and Walt and Hensa were following on, their faces set and pressured.

It was at that moment that the ramrod of the Bent Horn saw Dan. His gun swung up, and a bullet slapped into the cholla, then the whole herd roared between them. Dan leaped to his pony, and swerved away towards his partners. There was no need to continue the chase. The rustlers had scattered with the cattle, making their retreat for the Bent Horn.

'You got here in time to see the fun, Dan.' Curly grinned, wiping his face with the back of his hand. 'We sure gave them a belting. We thought they'd be back today, so we were ready.' Curly carried on, excited and breathless, 'We seen 'em rounding-up the herd. They were on our land. We strung logs across the draw, and when they drove up the valley we came at 'em from the flanks. Them steers just turned and started for home.'

Dan saw a trickle of blood from under Curly's hat. 'You hurt?'

Will was looking at his brother and smiled. 'One of 'em creased his block, so he blew him into the sky. He wanted to shoot 'em all.'

Dan looked at Curly and puffed his cheeks. 'Anybody else hurt?'

Hensa and Walt shook their heads silently. 'How about the Bent Horn lot?'

Will was still looking at his brother. 'You saw the three that came out. Nine went in.'

'Christ, you didn't kill six of 'em?'

Will looked serious. 'No. Two or three mutinied. They skedaddled out the end of the valley.'

Dan closed his eyes. 'One of the three that came my way was the ramrod. Curly's egg man. I couldn't make out the other two.'

'They were men Hayes brought in. Think how popular Curly's going to be, when he and Lummock find out.'

Curly rubbed at his smear of blood with a dirty forefinger. 'Don't go frettin' over me, Will.' He waved the carbine over his head. 'I can take care of myself.'

Dan saw something in Curly's temperament that worried him: a misplaced sense of bravado. Shades of Cotton Parker.

Will grumbled, 'It would suit me if we just rode into Eagle Spring and blew 'em apart. We know who's behind it all.'

Dan was feeling very uneasy, and he recognized their growing impatience. 'You've got to wait, Will, at least until I'm elected. We've got to do it right, or else nothing will be achieved. And you can keep that Spencer under control for a bit longer, Curly.'

8

Bad Night in the River Bend Saloon

Will and Curly were restless and edgy, and they needed some excitement. 'Come on, let's go to town,' Curly suggested.

The pair took a wagon into Eagle Spring, to the River Bend, looking for whiskey and a game of cards. For a while they stood at the bar joshing, until Carver Hayes was told of their appearance.

The saloon owner stormed from his office, and made straight for Will. 'You've got real nerve, coming in here, Glass. I'll put it down to stupidity. Now get out.'

Will smirked at Hayes's anger. 'You'll need a lot of help, when we decide not to.'

It was too much for Hayes. He took a step backwards, glaring at Will. He flexed his wrist, and a silver Derringer appeared in the palm of his hand. Curly was standing just behind Will, and he moved quickly. He pulled the Colt from Will's holster, and in one rounded movement fired a single shot into the black frock-coat.

As Hayes fell sideways against the bar, Will grabbed his gun from Curly. 'I think this is the end of us, Curly. Let's get out.'

The pair ran for the swing doors, but were stopped as Lummock and Jigger came through. Will was still holding his gun, and he shoved it at Lummock. 'Sorry, Sheriff, another mistake. We never came for this. Get outside, and you, Jigger.'

Curly took Jigger's gun, and together they marched the sheriff and marshal to the jail. Jigger was speechless with fear, and Lummock could only splutter with incoherent rage. Curly shoved them into a cell and tossed the keys into a cleaning pail. In less than a minute, they were hurtling their wagon away from the end of town.

For three days, Dan had been on the stump. It was while he was visiting one of the smaller ranches that he heard the news.

'Dan, I'm going to vote for you, but it's your brother and Curly who've got the right idea.'

'What idea's that?'

'Haven't you heard? Curly shot Carver Hayes last night. In the saloon.'

Dan was stunned. The rancher couldn't give him any more information, so he raced straight to Horse Creek. It was as he feared.

Will poured out the details, and pointed at Curly. 'It was this wildcat.'

Dan was totally exasperated. 'You locked the town's peace officers in the jail, and I'm running for election on the law and order tag?'

Will looked sheepishly at Curly. 'Yeah.'

Dan looked up to the sky. 'What the hell do I do now?'

Will's face lightened. 'We'll take the wagon into the hills, and stay lost.'

During the night the sheriff failed to

appear, and the following morning Walt rode to town. He discovered there was no warrant for Will or Curly. Lummock was too busy with the election.

Dan saw through that. If he was elected sheriff, he would have to arrest them both. There was no choice. If he didn't, he'd have to resign, but when he did, he'd be a lonely man.

Two days after that, in the early morning, Dan found Walt and Hensa getting ready to go to town. 'Looks like you're going to make a day of it. Don't forget to vote for me.'

Walt looked at Hensa, then back at Dan. 'Someone's gotta tell you.'

Dan shrank away from what was coming. 'Tell me what?'

'Will and Curly robbed Thomas Feigh at his home. The new deputy was out here an hour ago. Seems that somebody recognized Curly.'

'Robbed Feigh? Of what? What the hell are they doing?'

Walt shrugged. 'Damned if I know. Curly's running wild. They rode back here after midnight, then took off with the old tilbury wagon. Didn't say where they were going.'

Dan left for town immediately, almost running his pony into the ground. He stomped into the sheriff's office, and Lummock scowled from his desk. 'You got a lotta crust coming in here, Glass.'

Dan smiled coldly. 'I've heard a crazy tale from one of the Horse Creek boys. He told me Will and Curly are accused of holding up Feigh and his family last night.'

Lummock leaned back in his chair. 'That's the nub of it. And if you win the election you'll be bringing 'em in. Make it a speciality: relatives and friends, dead or alive.'

Dan walked to the door. 'How's Carver, Sheriff? And by the way, best of luck. The election is today, isn't it?'

Lummock's boots fell to the floor. 'Go to hell.'

9

The Town Decides

At midday, Eagle Spring was chock-a-block. The hitching rails and stables were packed with buckboards and horses. The town hadn't seen so much activity since Curly bought Horse Creek Ranch.

Dan nudged his pony along a line of men at the polling station. 'Looks like the entire county's turned out.'

Tommy Dinner spoke up. 'Too damn right. We're trying to make a difference. I expect you heard Hayes ain't gonna die. Maybe it won't go so hard on Curly when he's caught.'

Dan nodded thoughtfully, dismounted, and pushed his way into the hotel.

Goose Parker moved away from a group of

ranchers he was talking to. 'Congratulations, Dan. If all the talk means anything, you've won.'

Dan shook his head and smiled. 'Not yet, Mr Parker. I won't believe anything except the votes.'

Parker frowned. 'It's bad news about Curly Boyd though. There were plenty of witnesses besides the Feighs to testify that it was Will and Curly. As if your brother wasn't already in deep enough.'

Filena arrived to join her father, and Dan nodded politely. She stood to one side listening, and watching the movements of the town.

Parker asked, 'What do you aim to do about those two, if you're elected?'

Dan had been wondering himself. The prospect of having to bring in Curly and Will was grim. Any trial would be packed with Hayes's jurymen. 'I'll be expected to bring them in if I can find them.'

Filena started to say something, then changed her mind and walked away.

Dan glanced after her, and Parker caught the look in his eye. 'Something that Filena can't understand. Don't worry about it.'

Thomas Feigh then came in and introduced his daughter. 'This is the opposition candidate, Alex. He's tough and honest apparently, so be careful.' There was the faintest touch of sarcasm in his voice. Dan was surprised, because he hadn't known the banker had a daughter.

Alex's voice was unexpectedly low-pitched. She said, 'I'm delighted to meet you, Mr Glass. Father tells me you're a college man. I didn't expect to meet anyone above an eight grade in this dreadful country.'

Dan saw Filena watching them, so he didn't respond, or even say much.

Later, feeling cheerless and strangely detached, he took a stroll to the River Bend Saloon. He saw two of Hayes's men elbow their way into the street, and he wondered if something was in the wind. As the afternoon wore on, he became puzzled and aggravated by it. More employees of the gang were riding somewhere, stirred and determined.

By evening, the town was unusually peaceful, considering the day. Dan mentioned it to Jigger, who grinned slyly. 'I reckon they know it's you gunna be elected. So they're quiet, and timid as mouses.'

Dan looked at him with curiosity, and walked away from the jail. He remarked about it to the sheriff, but Lummock laughed openly. 'It's the Lock-'em-up Kid. 'Course there ain't no official count yet, but it sure looks like you're the town's next peace officer.'

Dan found Tommy Dinner, and told him of his unease.

'It's odd,' the rancher agreed. 'It's all too smug. They're up to something. I'll ask Zeke to find out what's going on.'

Dan sat alone in the hotel, forking chicken. He'd seen Hensa off to Horse Creek with Walt, who was a bit disgruntled at having to leave the festivities so early. He had to bolt his meat, since the harmonica player and two fiddlers were in the dining-room, tuning their instruments. The towns-people had gathered for the hoedown, and to hear the election returns. Women were in their best homespuns, or fancy city dress. The men had prudently hung up their guns and spurs, and their heads were plastered tight with wheel-grease.

In the middle of a dosido, a cowboy ran into the hotel and yelled, 'Dan Glass has been elected.'

The surrounding applause quelled the congratulations. A cowboy weaved his way through the dancers. He moved close to Dan and whispered, 'Curly's out back, and wants to see you.'

Dan threaded his way out of the hotel. He followed the man into the alley, where Curly appeared from the shadows.

He grabbed Dan by the arm, and spoke hurriedly. 'There's trouble on the timber-line. Hayes's men are damming the Piney. It was just luck that me and Will discovered it.

It's not finished, but when it is, the Piney'll flow south, along the old bed. It'll leave us dry as a bone.'

Dan looked hard at the cowboy, then back to Curly, 'Get some help, and take Walt. Take dynamite. That's our land.'

Curly drew back, and a few moments later Dan heard his horse tearing away. He saw Tommy Dinner outside the hotel, and told him what he'd heard.

Within minutes, worried, angry ranchers drifted away from the dance. The women were going to make the drive back to their ranches alone. The men rode for the hills in a furious, peppery group.

Lummock, Feigh and Goose Parker accompanied Dan to Judge Northwood's house where Dan took the oath of office.

Feigh looked smug, and he pulled an envelope from his pocket and handed it to Dan. 'This is an authority from the Department of the Interior. It approves the construction of a dam across the Piney. Read it over, Sheriff.'

Dan read the document, and then handed it to the judge. 'I'm no authority on this. Is it genuine?'

Judge Northwood nodded at him. 'I've already looked it over, Dan. Yes, it appears to be so.'

Parker had been watching the new sheriff. He said, 'That's a tough one to enforce, Dan, and I knew nothing about it. It's shameful, but legal. It'll ruin Horse Creek, and four or five other ranches.'

Dan felt the law against him, and he understood what he'd overheard that night, from above Feigh's office. The banker had ignored the Glass brothers' lease, and obtained government consent for the dam.

When the others had left, Dan asked what to do. The judge looked regretful. 'You can try taking out an injunction but that certainly requires the owner to put in an appearance. That's Curly Boyd, isn't it?'

Dan's shoulders sagged, and he studied the floor at his feet. He'd already sent Curly off with a sack of dynamite.

The judge considered Dan's position. 'You've picked that awkward space, in between justice and the law.'

'I expect you know what I'm going to do, Judge. I'm going to enforce the law. If people don't like it, they can change it.'

Dan walked to the sheriff's office, and saw the deputy drowsing in his chair. He lashed out at the man's feet. 'Pack your sock, Deputy. Come back in the morning and draw your pay.'

The man leaped to his feet, shaken but still drowsy. 'Why, what've I done?'

Dan ripped the badge from his vest. 'Nothing. But I don't like you, and I didn't appoint you. Now get out.'

Dan then stormed to the jail. He found Jigger playing clock patience, and said more or less the same to him. The marshal was another Hayes man.

From the marshal's office he went to the saloon and found the man he was looking for. 'Dorfmann, somebody said you're an honest man. That's a hell of a qualification at the moment, so I'm offering you a job with prospects. Town Marshal. Will you do it?'

Ham Dorfmann was the town's giant smith. 'Will I? Just give me a chance, Sheriff. It's the sort of employment I can make something of.'

Outside the livery stable, Dan found a deputy in Lemuel Grange, a friendly and enthusiastic young cowhand who was willing to try anything.

They rode to Horse Creek, where Dan spoke to Hensa. He explained what was going on up at the timberline, but asked him to stay at the ranch.

Within an hour, Dan and Grange set out for the foothills of the Ozarks. They were on fresh horses, and they racked through the parched gullies that led to the higher course of the Piney.

Grange was peering up to the first of the pine stands. 'What you figgering to do when we get to that dam? Folks are mighty troubled at this water business, and that was a big passel of anger that left town.'

The sheriff nudged his horse gently. 'Maybe convince them of the pitfalls of taking on the law.' He smiled at his deputy.

10

The Dammed Piney

They'd used moonlight to travel by, and the air was clean and cold. The two men climbed through the timberline, the horses' hooves clicking and rattling against the scree. Dan knew the approximate location of the dam, and headed to the nearest run of the stream.

Lemmy Grange lolled in his saddle. 'Lack of sleep's getting me. I've been dreaming of apple pie. We taking a meal camp before we get there?'

Dan had ridden mostly in silence, wondering how he'd deal with the situation. He was responsible for it.

'I don't feel like breakfast.' He stared grimly ahead of him.

They picked their way along the shale bed of the creek, icy water sucking and swirling at the feet of their horses. When they could no longer follow the course of the stream, they climbed out through a pine-covered ridge, and Dan pointed into the gully below.

'There's the dam. It looks quiet.'

They close-reined the horses, and edged sideways down the side of the gully. The dam was a clumsy structure, but sturdy enough to divert the course of the river. From behind a pine stump, Lummock appeared. Then Will, with an anxious Tommy Dinner.

Will yelled out. 'Howdy, Sheriff. How does it feel to have the law behind you?'

Then Dinner shouted, 'It's about time you came, Dan. We're ready to blow that litter apart.'

Lummock turned to face Dinner and Will. 'You don't understand, boys. The sheriff's here to protect the dam. We got the authority of government to build.'

Curly was behind and to one side of Will

and Dinner. He saw the set of Dan's face, and read it correctly. He edged back into thick bracken.

Dan said, as calmly as he could, 'I was mistaken about the dam. Lummock's right. They have the authority, and if you blow it, I'll have to arrest you.'

Dinner exploded, 'Like hell!'

Will turned to his brother. 'You're letting them get away with this?'

The sheriff nodded. 'They've got the cards. There's nothing I can do.'

While Lummock smirked, Curly had worked his way to within a few feet of the dam. The ranchers were emerging from cover, and standing dejectedly alongside Will and Tommy Dinner.

Curly was hunkered down, rolling a cigarette. He was watching the faces of the dam builders, and Lummock. He struck a match and, taking a few puffs of his cigarette, he let his hand dangle loose at his side. Several times he glanced sideways at the ground, then suddenly he leaped to his feet, and yelled, 'Run for it! I've lit the fuse!'

Hands flew for guns even as the men were running, diving for safety. A rifle shot reverberated through the gully, followed immediately by gunfire that crashed and bounced off the rocks and trees. Dan and his deputy were caught in a deadly crossfire.

As Grange fell from his horse and crawled for shelter, Dan watched the wisping smoke from the lighted fuse. Then, in spite of the pelt of bullets, he sprang, crushing and smothering the fizzing flame with the hooves of his horse. He whooped with emotion, and spun away, making a grab for Grange's shotgun. He fired both barrels, and through the sudden following silence, yelled for a ceasefire.

As the shooting faltered, Curly staggered, grinning, from behind a pile of chopped timber. But there was something wrong and, as Dan watched, the grin stretched into a grimace as Curly took a small step forward. A dark stain grew on the front of his shirt, and Dan swore quietly, as he ran to the man who was crumpling to the ground. Curly keeled onto his side, and his eyes searched despairingly across the flattened, muddy grass.

Will came up, and reached out for his friend. Dan said nothing; there was no need: Curly wouldn't have wanted any natural, or instinctive comforting, and they both knew he'd be staying where he was. Walt brought a canteen of water and held it to his lips. But nothing moved, and Curly's eyes weren't focusing any more.

One of the ranchers laid a saddle blanket beside Dan. 'We can get him back to the doc, can't we?'

Dan was going to say *no*, when Lummock called out to him 'It can't stop the dam being finished, Sheriff.'

Dan and Will looked across at him. The total silence was overwhelming. Dan still couldn't find any words, and his mouth trembled. His eyes clouded, and he gripped his hands together, tight. Will was staring at his younger brother seeking assurance and calm, and Lummock remained alive for a while longer.

There was sudden fear among the ranchers and the men building the dam, the fear of the Glass brothers, and their ability to dispense retribution. It created a situation, and neither camp wanted to continue the gunfight.

Walt considered a tote between two horses to carry the body back, but the terrain was impassable. Dan knew some appropriate words, a short prayer for dead soldiers, and they used it to bury Curly. It was at the headwater, above a ridge that overlooked Horse Creek Ranch.

The ranchers left for their homes. Curly had never meant much until now, until he'd given his life to give *them* water. But it was a death blow to most of the smaller ranchers. It looked like the cartel had gained a stranglehold on the entire county, and many of them suddenly regretted their votes for Dan Glass. They'd thought he'd be with them, *regardless* of being sheriff.

Judge Northwood listened to the account of the gunfight and Curly's death, then handed Dan a small packet.

'Curly asked me to hold these letters. It was in the event of anything happening to him. The ranch never really belonged to him, Dan. It never lost the name of William Malachy Glass as inheritor. Curly just paid the money. If Will dies, or gets himself killed, then it goes to you. The Sedalia City Bank holds Curly's will, and the land documents.'

Dan walked back to the sheriff's office. He unlocked the door, went in, and locked it again from the inside. He pushed open the door to the bunk room, looked morosely at Will, and handed him the letters.

Will breathed hard. 'I'd better be on my way. You'll have to start serving them warrants soon.' He stood and rubbed his thumb across Dan's badge of office. 'And by the way, those papers me and Curly took from Feigh, they're probably still in his saddle pouch. They meant nothing to me, but Curly thought different. Find them, and have a look.'

'Where will you go, Will?'

The reluctant fugitive smiled sourly. 'I promised to give you a free rein, but Curly changes something. 1 can't leave that alone. If you need help, see Walt. He'll find me. And keep an eye on the ranch. It belongs to me, don't forget.' He squeezed his brother's shoulder, and was gone.

Dan stepped back into the office, and looked through Curly's saddle pouch. Then he looked out the window, towards the setting sun.

Much later, he had two visitors, Pole Lummock and Thomas Feigh at his most pompous. 'We heartily approve of your actions at the timberline, Sheriff, but there are also one or two other things to consider. We ought to make it clear.'

It was all Dan could do to stop slapping them around. The banker sensed it, and h'mm h'mmed. 'There are still warrants on a number of people, and it's up to you to bring them to justice. You know who we're talking about.'

Dan smiled grimly. 'Yes. And I know who we're *not* talking about as well. Your payroll of scum.'

Lummock twitched, and Dan spat the words with contempt. 'I was elected on a platform of law and order, not the violation you dispatch. If Will shows up, I'll take him in, or try to. But maybe I'll start nearer home. Clearing out the River Bend Saloon for a start. Lummock did little about it.'

Feigh nodded. 'Valuable sentiments, Sheriff. Eagle Spring will be well rid of the sort.'

Dan pulled his gun, and slammed it on the table. '*Valuable sentiments,* you hypocrite! You're the *sort* we'll all be well rid of. I'd empty every jail in Missouri in exchange for banging up you two.'

Dan pushed the handgun deep and low into Feigh's stomach, and with his other hand, he grabbed at Lummock's throat. He looked him close in the eye. 'Get out, Lummock. Take him with you, and stay a long way away from me.'

When the two men had gone, Dan waited for his anger to subside. He went back to the window. It was dark now, and the peaks of the Ozarks were as black as the night.

'Well I told them, Curly. You'd have shot them, wouldn't you?'

11

Loneliness and the Law

Deeply morose, Dan rode to Goose Pond. He cracked his heels across the timbers of the stoop as a loud notice of his calling.

Goose Parker came to the door, and swung it wide, with a look of welcome. 'Hello, Dan. It's getting late, what can we do for you?'

'Nothing, Mr Parker. I've brought bad news.'

Filena came from another room. She saw the cloud in Dan's eyes and looked to her father to say something.

The rancher put out a hand for Dan to enter the house. 'Tell me. What's happened?'

'Curly Boyd was shot and killed, up on the timberline. We buried him there. I thought

117

maybe you'd like to know.'

He'd got it out, short, but then he told them of the fight at the dam, and all the while he could see Filena silently arranging her feelings and response.

'You sent him to his death, as sure as your name's Glass.'

Parker stepped in as gently as he could. 'Dan was doing his job, Filena. A job we asked him to do, elected him to do.'

Filena looked at Dan, her eyes slightly closed. 'The Glass brothers of Eagle Spring. A killer outlaw, and a killer sheriff.'

Dan picked up his hat, and ran the brim between his fingers. 'I told Curly to organize the ranchers, and dynamite the dam. I told him the law would defend their rights. But there was something I didn't know, and because of that Curly died. I can't undo it now. I just came to tell you.'

Filena stood up. There was no sympathy in her voice. 'You came to tell us the ranch is yours again.' She turned her back, and stalked from the room.

Parker shook his head. 'I'm sorry, Dan. I sometimes despair of what this land is doing.'

'It's not the land, Mr Parker, it's the people.'

As Dan climbed onto his pony, a figure approached the hitching rail.

'Too bad about the "Buffalo Bug", Sheriff. The children in town'll miss him.'

Dan looked down at Cotton Parker. His mind played with two or three responses. If there'd been one, and for the sake of Curly, it would have been the end of Parker. Parker gritted his teeth and backed off slowly. He held his hands out to Dan, acknowledging his stupidity.

Tommy Dinner had suggested a service for Curly, and they'd waited nearly a week for the travelling minister. The short ceremony was held outside the hotel, and a few ranchers came to pay their overdue respects. Just after the bank clock had struck midday, Dan caught sight of the paint pony sidling in from the end of town. Others saw it too, and they looked to the sheriff for a response.

Lummock and Feigh stepped to the balustrade that fronted the hotel. Dan saw them, and swore to himself.

The ex-sheriff looked down at Dan. 'Your brother's arrived, Glass. Arrest him.'

Will dropped from his horse, and looked warily around him. He pulled a Winchester from his saddle sheath and, while looking at Lummock, spoke quietly. 'We want a peaceful service. No need for any trouble. Walt, take his gun, and frisk the banker. Dan, please give Hensa your gunbelt.'

Lummock's face turned purple with rage as Walt and Hensa stepped forward, and Feigh puffed with indignation as Walt felt his corpulence. The ranchers shuffled uneasily, as the minister stood shocked, waiting.

Will looked up into the eyes of Lummock and Feigh. Two men who felt the relief of living, as they backed into the hotel.

When the minister finished a hurried prayer, the ranchers began to drift off, and Will spoke quietly.

'Sorry 'bout the gun, Dan, but I need to talk to you without being arrested.'

The small group walked to the corral and Will beckoned to Tommy Dinner. He took the Smith & Wesson back from Hensa. 'It's for appearances.' He winked at his brother. 'I've been back to the dam. They've finished the building, and the water's flowing to the old channel. In a week this range'll be bone dry, and in less than a month, the herds'll be dying. What're you aiming to do about it, Dan? It's not just Horse Creek I'm worried about.'

Dan held the tips of his fingers to a nosing mule. 'They had the authority to build the dam. The judge is in touch with Washington, but it may be weeks before we have permission to blow it.'

Tommy Dinner nodded gloomily. 'He's right, Will. You know it. I'm digging meself a well.'

Will exploded. 'Hell, Tommy! Your cattle will die, and it'll kill *you* in the end.'

Dan watched the mule as it kicked the hard-packed ground. He was regretting now that he was sheriff. He thought he could give the weaker ranchers the strength of the law. But it was making barriers. He moved away from the fence.

'Will, you promised you'd give me a free hand if and when I was elected. Keep your word.'

Will laughed. 'I always keep my word. Don't champ your bit. I'll give you a month to get water to the ranchers, legal-like, and then I'll go and blow the dam myself. One month, Dan.'

Dinner nodded in agreement. 'That's fair enough. The cattle can make it for three, maybe four weeks.'

The five men walked back to the hotel, and Will handed back Dan's gunbelt. He smiled. 'You're too good and law-abiding for me.'

Moments later Will rode off, heading

north, and Dan headed for his office.

For the next week he was too busy with his duties to pay much attention to the ranchers. With the help of his deputy, Grange, and the enthusiastic town marshal Dorfmann, Eagle Spring made a start to clean itself up. Lummock kept out of his way, as did Carver Hayes, who'd finally recovered from Curly's bullet.

He'd seen little of the banker, but one afternoon Alex stopped him on the street, and chided him for not paying her a visit. Unlike the banker, she was open and genuinely interested in Dan's duties. He told her that Lemuel Grange was off to Sedalia as they walked slowly to his office.

Alex smiled naïvely. 'I've never known a real sheriff before. You're not a bit like I imagined.'

He laughed. 'You've been reading those store dime-novels.'

They walked into the office, and Dan looked around him. 'Very few of us become as wealthy as your father.' He looked at her with as much cynicism as he dared. 'There's disease and rustling and drought that takes its toll. And as for the law... If I can't get water down to the ranches in a couple of weeks, there are some who'll take the law into their own hands.'

'You mean your brother, don't you? Why is it that you hate my father?'

'It's not *hate,* Alex. Your father and his colleagues only have a commercial interest in the land. If the cattle don't get water, the ranchers are forced to sell up. Your father buys them out, re-routes the water, and owns half the county. I don't want to see all my father's work end up like that.'

The next morning Dan rode north through the bluffs, then dropped to the flats of the Dinner spread. The lack of water had already cracked the land, and Tommy had fixed up a well-drilling rig. With the aid of his wife and a cow hand, he was toiling in the arid soil, but when Dan rode up, his grey eyes brightened. 'Any news, Sheriff?'

Dan shook his head. 'Not a word yet, Tommy.'

The old rancher became niggly. 'Will was right. We should have fought it out.' He kicked at a piece of timber. 'Two weeks now we been sweating at this job, and we ain't got near water.'

At the Redwing, the situation was just as bad. But, unlike his neighbour, Hector Redwing was of a fighting mind. Dan tried to tell him that it would only work against him, but after twenty minutes, he knew he hadn't convinced the man.

When Dan recrossed the bluff, he would have been even more worried if he'd turned and seen the activity. Two men rode off with rifles and shotguns, and Redwing drove horses in from the range. Two big pack-mules were loaded with provisions, and several canvas pouches were securely tied to their flanks. Then, they were covered with oilskin, and padded with saddle blankets to prevent any jolting.

12

Guns at the Timberline

The next morning Dan rode south with his deputy. They stopped at the Goose Pond, and Parker's foreman, Charlie Chalk, grinned when he saw them. 'Have you boys seen any water from the Piney lately? It's tough on Horse Creek, but that stream's god-blessed here.'

Dan and Grange rode on. A few miles further south they crossed the new course of the Piney. There was a head of water in the stream, and it was flowing swiftly towards the Bent Horn and ranches beyond. A green carpet was rolling across the earth, and the grasses were thickening with moisture.

Dan and his deputy drew in at the Bent Horn, and the bald-headed ramrod met them at the corral. Dan noticed how their cattle had taken on weight since his last visit, and remarked on it.

Egg man laughed. 'We're taking some of the meat off your cows, and slapping it around ours.'

Dan swung his horse's head away. There was only one or two of the original ranch owners left. The new men were mercenaries, who knew and felt nothing for the land or cattle.

The sheriff and his deputy cantered back to Eagle Spring. It was Saturday night, but only the River Bend Saloon, and the hotel were ablaze with lights.

Grange said, 'Where is everybody? It's more lively in Boot Hill.'

Dan had noticed the quietness too, with no more than a dozen horses on the street. Finding that Ham Dorfmann was not at the jail, they strolled to the saloon.

Carver Hayes was standing at the bar, and he turned to face the lawmen.

'What the hell's happening, Glass? I've

never known this town so dead.'

Dan shook his head. 'I was wondering the same thing. I thought you'd know. Trouble at the dam site, maybe?'

They heard a horse snorting, and pounding outside the saloon, and Dan muttered, 'Someone's in a hurry.'

They reached the sheriff's office as a rider was stumbling to the ground. Dan and Lem grabbed at his cape, and carried him inside. He'd taken a bullet in his right shoulder, and Grange went for the town doctor. Dan persuaded the doctor not to administer any painkiller. The rider had brought trouble, and Dan wanted to know about it. Before Heggarty began to probe for the bullet, the man's eyes opened and he looked up into Dan's face.

'It's the dam, Sheriff. The ranchers are going to destroy it. Lummock's holed up in the gully. There's no way out. Some are wounded. Take the doc, here. They'll need him.'

Dan asked Grange to find fresh horses. He

hurried to the hotel, and then the saloon, seeking a posse. But the few men in town weren't inclined to get mixed up in a gunfight.

Hayes sneered, 'If you hadn't thrown your weight around in here, I could have raised you a posse. You're on your own, Sheriff.'

Dan didn't waste any more time and, with Grange, rode to the west of Horse Creek, then into the foothills. In some ways, it was a reprise of their first ride together, except this time, a waxing moon lit their way.

The town's doctor had been slow, and they hadn't waited. He was probably an hour's ride behind them. Eventually the moon dropped, and shadows merged into blackness ahead of them. For another three hours they climbed steadily upward, and it wasn't until the first streaks of dawn appeared, that they drew in their horses.

In the gully, the dam was clouded in low swirling mist. There was someone hidden high on the edge. A voice cut through the crisp, still air. 'It's the sheriff. He can't stop us now, boys. Pepper that dam.'

The ensuing gunfire rasped and clattered along the gully, and from the barrier of the dam came a volley of answering flashes.

Grange yelled, 'What we gonna do now, Sheriff? There ain't nobody to help, 'cept those behind the dam, and they're a mite busy.'

Dan looked casually across the gully, and down to the dam. 'We'll sit and wait awhile.'

They dismounted, tied their horses into the pines, and Dan sat and pondered the crossfire. He'd recognized the voice; it was Hector Redwing.

The light spread, but fog still curled into the narrow gully. Dan pinched out the end of a cigarette, and stood up. 'The doc should be near, Lem. Better walk back and see. I'll find Lummock.'

Grange voiced his thinking. 'I wouldn't. I heard what happened to Curly Boyd. A stray bullet wasn't it?'

Dan shrugged. 'There're wounded men behind that dam. I've got to try and stop

131

this.' He looked sharply at his deputy. 'I think it's what I get paid for.'

Dan edged his way along the gully. Through the mist, a ricocheted bullet buzzed by his ear, and he ducked on impulse. His foot slipped, and he clattered into a boulder. His rifle fell to the stream, and a nerve twisted him around. With drawn guns, Hector Redwing and Tommy Dinner emerged from the bankside mist. Redwing stepped down into the stream and retrieved the Winchester, then removed Dan's revolver from his holster.

'You weren't invited, so don't spoil the party, Sheriff. We don't mean you any harm, you know that. Get back to the ridge, while we blow the dam.'

Dinner motioned with his Colt, and Redwing looked back along the stream bed and across the gully. 'Where's that deputy of yours?'

Dan sloshed from the shallow water. 'Search me. Is my brother up here?'

In a glum voice, Tommy Dinner said. 'No,

Dan. He promised you, remember? He was here last night though.'

Dan had no doubt that Will would keep his word. But as he cast an eye around the pines and rocks above him, he felt a beguiling protection. He turned to Dinner. 'Unless you give this up, and clear out of here, I'll... Tommy, you know the law. You elected me to enforce it.'

The rancher shrugged, and looked across at Redwing. 'We might as well be in jail as broke. We're going to raise those logs, up to the vultures. You can watch it from the ridge, Dan. You don't have much say in it.'

Four men then drifted out of the trees. One was Grange, another Doc Heggarty, and behind them, two men with lowered rifles.

Grange leered at Dinner and Redwing, then looked resignedly at Dan.

'Appears we're not wanted here. Might as well let 'em fight it out.'

The doctor was allowed to tend the wounded, and Dan and his deputy were led back to the ridge.

As the sun climbed higher, it burned off the mist and firing broke out again. 'Dan, asked Tommy Dinner, 'how many men are with Lummock?'

'A dozen maybe, not sure. They're scattered around the dam. The water's not that deep, but there's already a depth in the old channel.'

Dinner swung the tip of his rifle up to the peaks. 'With the high rain from last week, there's a head of water on the way. They won't *need* their dam for long. It's got to go now.'

Dan realized why the ranchers refused to wait. When the Piney threw its course, it would have to be dammed again, to throw it back.

Dan and Lem Grange squatted on the ridge and watched the fight below them. If Lummock had brought ten men, there weren't more than seven left, probably less. They couldn't endure a long fight, and there'd be no reinforcement.

The sun's heat began to power down. It

didn't bother the ranchers much, hidden in the pines and rocky sides of the gully, but it was harsh on the defenders of the dam.

Dan said, 'Tommy, I want to speak to Hec. Can you get him up here? Quickly.'

Fifteen minutes later, a cowhand returned with Redwing. Dan stood up and pointed down into the gully. 'There's three Lummock men wounded down there. Send someone to bring them out with the doc. You're no killer, Hec.'

As three men slanted their way down the gully, a withering fire suddenly poured into the dam. One of the ranchers was trying to reach the dam under cover of the guns, and in his hand he held two sticks of fizzing dynamite. He got to within thirty feet of the barricade, when Lummock's men ripped three or four bullets into his back. As he fell, the rancher stiff-armed the dynamite into a low curling arc. One stick fell short into the stream, but the other bounced once, before wedging itself into the stacked timbers. It was a small charge, and there were no deaths, but the blast spouted water, wood, stones and mud. A yell broke from the ranchers, and a final fusillade broke against the dam.

A trickle of water oozed through, then more, until the stream began to muscle its way between the tangled logs and timbers.

Dan heard, then saw Hec Redwing shout. A rider was coming along the stream, and Dan could see the bright gleam of a marshal's star against a black coat. Four men were following on, and Dan recognized them immediately: Goose Parker and his foreman, Charlie Chalk, Hensa and Judge Northwood.

Redwing splashed down the stream to meet them, and Dan saw him shake hands with the marshal. With Tommy Dinner still close, Dan and his deputy were escorted down to the bed of the gully.

'Goodday, Sheriff,' the marshal greeted Dan. 'Jim Challonde, US Marshal out of Sedalia.'

Dan looked into a brutally hard face, but

the marshal was relaxed and in command.

'The judge has an order from the Department of the Interior. It authorizes me to blow this dam to hell. So get up a flag, and wave that crowbait out of here. It's hot, and I don't take to this kinda work.'

Lummock and his men moved out and away from the broken dam.

'You're all too late, Marshal. They've done their worst.'

The fighting men looked to the splintering timbers as water flowed back to the old stream bed.

The marshal looked at Dan. 'Hmm. A mite premature, but I'm satisfied.' He then looked sternly at Redwing. 'As for you, mister, you're not the sort of man who gives the right time.'

Dan had his gunbelt returned, and he mounted his horse. He talked briefly with the marshal, and Challonde nodded in agreement.

Dan stood in his stirrups, the marshal on one side, his deputy on the other. He held up his hand to the ranchers. 'The water's running back to your ranches, but you've a debt to settle. You're all under arrest. Unhook your gunbelts. Deputy Grange'll gather them up.

Tommy Dinner was the first to respond. 'Try and take me to jail, Sheriff.'

The US marshal's Colt suddenly appeared in his hand, and Dan gently gripped his Smith & Wesson. 'I've asked the marshal to shoot the first man who makes a move for his gun. He assures me he will.'

The lawmen were convincing enough, and the ranchers and cowhands dropped their handguns and rifles to the ground.

During the surrender, a large muscle of a man eased off from the group and slipped into the fringe of dense pines. Dan saw him, but gave no sign. It was Ham Dorfmann, the town marshal and ex-foreman of the Redwing ranch. His regard for a former boss had brought him into the fight, but he wasn't after compromising the town sheriff, or losing his new job.

13

Judge Northwood's Trial

They were a sorry bunch, the men who rode down from the mountains that afternoon, under the eye of the sheriff and the US marshal. The jail of Eagle Spring was small, and already occupied, so Dan settled for holding three ranch owners. He allowed the hands to return to their ranches under guarantee of a reappearance. Jim Challonde was staying over for the noon stage to Sedalia. It would leave as Judge Northwood's trial started.

Due to the amount of local interest, and number of defendants, the hotel dining-room was requisitioned as a courthouse. Carver Hayes had his hired thugs to face-off friends of the ranchers, and fearing trouble, the sheriff and his deputy were barring all weapons from the hotel.

Before proceedings commenced, the judge asked to see Ham Dorfmann in private. 'How many can your jail take, Marshal?'

Ham thought it might be for something else, so he answered quickly. 'Six, Judge. Ten, if I'm pushed.'

The judge looked curiously impressed. 'How many have you got cooped up there at the moment?'

'Ten, Judge.'

'Thank you, Marshal, that's all I need to know at the moment.'

Tommy Dinner took the stand first, to give a simple but faltering outline of the difficulties he'd had in obtaining water for his cattle. Then, twelve other defendants followed in rapid succession, their stories about starving and thirsty herds, equally brief and moving.

It was late afternoon when the judge rapped for order. He glowered at the prisoners, cleared his throat, and drummed his fingers on a law book. 'In this case, and according to state law, I have the right to determine sentence. Therefore, and due to the seriousness of the charge, I will *not* impose the minimum sentence.' The judge looked across the makeshift courtroom. 'The accused will stand to hear their sentences.'

The defendants shuffled uneasily to their feet, and the judge flicked his gaze across their distraught faces. 'I impose the maximum of six months in jail, or a one-thousand-dollar fine.'

Protestations and curses mingled with immediate jeers from the Hayes camp. Dan was shocked, although he tried hard to disguise it. The judge banged for order, and Dan and his deputy shouted for quiet.

Judge Northwood folded his hands across the law book, and addressed the ranch men. 'From what *I* know, there's none of you able to raise the fine, and no doubt you'll plump for the jail sentence. Nevertheless, and as most of *you* know, the jail can't make that

141

accommodation. I'm therefore suspending sentence. And may I remind you, gentlemen, that you are all bound-over for six months. And that means, *keep the peace.*'

It took a moment for the judge's sentence to filter through, then a soft cheer rolled through the courtroom. The dam had been freed, and so had they.

Dan returned to his office. Goose Parker called by, and invited him to dinner at the ranch. 'It's none of my business, Dan, but I don't like the way things have meted out between you and Filena. The girl's obviously sorry for some of the things she's said.'

The sun had dropped behind the Ozarks when the sheriff dismounted at the corral of the Goose Pond. He uncinched his pony and walked slowly towards the ranch house. There was something lurking unsettled at the back of his mind.

Filena Parker was waiting for him on the stoop, and he approached doubtfully. She held out her hand, and gave a brief smile. 'It was good of you to come, Dan. I didn't think you would. That night, I didn't mean what I said. We all liked Curly. He made me laugh with his enthusiasm. He was so open, almost childlike. I was wrong, very wrong, and I'm sorry for what I said.'

Dan thought there might be a chance for him after all. 'No, you were right. It's not *what* you said, it was you *saying* it. If it hadn't been for me, Curly might be alive now.'

They exchanged misgivings for a while, mending some fences. Dan was going to tell her that there wasn't a lot *childish* about Curly Boyd, but didn't.

Dan, although seemingly attentive, was distracted while they ate. There was still something at the back of his mind. It ran from talking about Curly, but he couldn't put a finger on it, and wanted to be away.

It was late when he left the Parkers. He'd actually stayed because of the excellence of the meal. There was nothing else more immediately pressing, until he recalled the problem on his mind. It was the packet of papers stolen from the banker. They'd lain in his desk since Curly's death, and for some reason he'd forgotten them.

At two in the morning, Dan turned his pony into the livery stable. He went straight to his office, where Grange was sound asleep in the bunk room. He lit the lamp, and pulled the envelope from his desk drawer. At first it didn't make any sense, but as he reread, it came clearer. It was Thomas Feigh's record of affairs of the cartel, and it included Cotton Parker's involvement.

Dan stared into his flickering desk lamp. The papers must be damaging evidence, and with an unbiased jury and a decent attorney, it might be sufficient to convict the whole group. To his knowledge there'd been no obvious attempt to get the papers back, even with a dated inventory, and references to cattle. Dan could remember some of the dates. They coincided with Horse Creek

144

losing yearlings. He decided what he would have to do, and locked the papers back in his desk. He had enough evidence now, with the written confession from Philun Pegg.

His eyes pricked for sleep. It could all wait a few hours. He stretched himself on the office cot and, as he drifted into sleep, a final thought went through his head: Carver Hayes might be a tough one to arrest with a murder charge facing him.

14

The Spencer Carbine

The same morning, Dan obtained the warrant for Carver Hayes's arrest, and with Dorfmann and Grange walked into the River Bend Saloon.

Knowing that Hayes kept late hours, he reckoned on the saloon owner still being in his bed, and not even the barman was about. There was only the Chinaman pot-boy, lazily brooming up the night's mess.

The sheriff asked where Hayes was, but the Chinaman shook his head. 'China don't know.' And that was all Dan got out of the old man.

The door to Hayes's office opened, and someone Dan knew as Swinton Dobbs, thrust his unshaven face around the door.

'What the hell do you lot want?'

His eyes were bloodshot and bagged. Dan knew his breed; a mercenary gunman whom he'd been unable to find in the circulars. He'd arrived in Eagle Spring shortly after the sheriff's clear-up. Dan questioned him, and the gunman sniffed arrogantly.

'The Chinaman told you: Mr Hayes ain't here. What you want him for?'

Dan shot a glance at his deputy, then pushing the man aside, he stepped quickly through the door. But the gunman and China were right. Hayes's bed, in the through-room of his office, hadn't been slept in. With a promise that they'd meet again, the gunman bade Dan farewell.

Dan saddled his pony at the livery stable, then rode back to Goose Pond. He rode fast to the ranch house, and both Parker and Filena stepped out to meet him. The sheriff hadn't meant to reveal his findings, or plans, but with Cotton involved, he felt that it was right to give Parker a fuller picture.

Parker's face remained calm, but pained.

'I'm not one for asking favours, Dan, but could you consider giving the boy a chance to square himself? Some of it's down to me. I should have noticed something.'

The sheriff was determined. 'He'll have the right to a defence, Mr Parker, the same as anyone else. He'll be brought to trial, and it'll be up to a jury to decide if he's worth that chance, not me.'

Dan felt the chilling silence from Filena. He'd already said too much. He should have kept his mouth shut. Parker would probably warn off his son.

'Where is this *evidence* you have?' Filena eventually asked.

Dan looked at her sharply. 'A jury will meet for a special session. The evidence will be there.'

Filena glanced at a partially closed door that led off the main room. Dan caught the deceptive movement, but thought little of it, only later, as he rode back towards town. There was a lone horseman, cutting across the north range of Goose Pond.

He hitched his pony to the rail, and walked into his office. His deputy turned in his chair, and looked up surprised, but grinning. 'This'll interest you, Sheriff. Look here.' He handed Dan a copy of the *Fort Scott News*.

Dan read an inside page of the Kansas newspaper. Pole Lummock, out of Stover County, Missouri, had been appointed Deputy United States Marshal. In an interview, the new deputy was reported to be 'taking immediate steps to clean up the border'. According to Lummock, time was running out for lawlessness and outlawry, Among those on a Wanted list was Will Glass.

'I think Will would like to see this.' Dan tore a clipping, folded it, and shoved it under his hat. 'Has Hayes come back?'

Grange shook his head. 'Nope. He'll be on the border with Lummock, celebrating.'

With no pressing law business, Dan decided to ride out to the ranch to see Hensa, but as he pulled out of the livery stable he met him. He was with Walt, in the tilbury wagon, carrying supplies. Dan looped his pony to the tailgate, and tucked-up amongst the grain sacks. He brought the two of them up to date, and connivingly gave Walt the news clipping.

It was dark when the wagon topped the low bluffs around Horse Creek, but they could all see light flickering in the ranch house. Hensa said. 'Who's in the house?'

Walt immediately reined in. 'That's odd, unless—'

He stopped suddenly, and glanced side-ways at Dan. 'No, it ain't Will.'

Dan peered through the dark. 'Looks like three horses.'

Walt and Hensa dropped from their seats, and Dan rolled from the tailgate. Walt pulled out Curly's big carbine, and Hensa checked his Colt. The three men looked at each other, then walked steadily on to the ranch house. Dan and Hensa approached the front entrance, and Walt moved around the side of the building.

Away from any light, Walt stumbled into a feed can. The stock of his long gun banged against the hollow tin, and within seconds a shotgun blasted out from a front window. It was followed immediately by a hail of gunfire pouring from all the ranch-house windows.

Dan yelled, 'This is the sheriff, Daniel Glass. Come out and live, or stay in and die.' He knew the amount of damage he'd inflict was close to an empty threat. It was, arguably, his own house.

A contemptuous yell came from the men inside. They were obviously thinking the same thing, and more bullets stormed around Dan and Hensa.

Dan beckoned to Hensa. 'Can you keep 'em busy while I get to the back?'

Hensa looked calmly at the sheriff. 'I don't think I can, no. This is for me to do. I'll go up through the storm-trap. Two or three minutes. Stay here and look out for Walt, he's still round that side somewhere.' He moved away before Dan could say another word.

Walt was crouching in the dark. He'd backed away from the house, and waited thirty feet from where Dan was calmly standing. Hensa had disappeared into the storm-trap, and there was only sporadic fire from the windows. The men inside had decided not to waste their ammunition.

Walt called softly, 'What's Hensa up to?'

Dan held up the flat of his hand, indicating for him to wait steady. He listened to the horses at the hitching rail. They were stamping and whinnying, badly spooked by the unseen clamour. But suddenly, from inside the ranch house he heard the sharp noise of the Navy Colt. There were two shots in rapid succession, followed by an agonized yell. Then a moment of silence, before Hensa called for him and Walt.

With guns at the ready, the two men came loping into the room. Walt remained in the doorway, and Dan edged around the side wall. One man was crumpled by the window gripping a Colt, but quickly dying. Another sat propped against the leg of a table. It was Charlie Chalk. His face was set with the grind of pain from the wound deep in his shoulder, blood oozing across his vest. Standing in the middle of the room, his face twisted with rage and fists clenched, was Cotton Parker.

Dan looked hard at Hensa, and tried to recall something Curly had said about him. Then he stepped across to Parker, and with the back of his hand whipped a savage smack across his face. 'This is my house you're violating, Parker. What are you doing here?'

Parker spat a crude epithet and remained silent.

Walt said, 'We'd better take Charlie into town, Dan. He's losing blood.'

'Not yet.'

Parker's face was quickly draining of colour, and his eyes were shifting from one face to another. 'Go to hell, all of you.'

Cotton Parker had the vocabulary and reserve of Philun Pegg. Unexpectedly his foot swung up, and the toe of his boot caught Dan in the groin. Dan grunted, and doubled back in pain, and both men went crashing into Hensa. Parker snatched at Dan's holster, and then staggered sideways. His thumb clawed back the hammer of the Smith & Wesson, and he levelled it down towards Dan.

There was one great blast of a shot from the doorway, and a thick coil of smoke rose from the big carbine in Walt's hand. The impact of the .52 bullet took Cotton Parker off his feet, and he was dead before he hit the far wall.

Walt turned the barrel of the gun towards the floor. 'Christ, Dan, I didn't mean to–'

Dan stooped painfully, and picked up his gun from Parker's lifeless fingers.

'That's what that gun does, Walt. It's not interested in warnings.'

Walt looked towards Hensa. 'I wasn't aiming to *kill* him. But when I seen him point that gun–'

Hensa took the carbine from Walt's grasp. 'You just saved *all* our lives Walt.'

Dan stared hard at the body. 'What was he after?'

Charlie Chalk groaned. 'He said you had something that would send us to jail. We had to get it.'

Then the sheriff understood. Goose Parker, or Filena, had told Cotton of the evidence. Possible even, that Hayes had put him up to it.

Walt turned suddenly, and looked into the night. 'Somebody's coming.'

Dan stopped staring at Cotton, and banged the heel of his hand against his forehead. 'That'll be Grange. Hayes is probably back. I've got a warrant for his arrest. Walt, can you and Hensa load Charlie onto his horse?'

Grange drew rein, and ran up the steps. He came through the door and looked around him. His mouth started working, but it was his eyes that were asking the questions. Dan decided to leave it for later.

Charlie was lifted onto his horse, and Parker was laid in the wagon with his horse hitched on behind. The riders moved south, back towards the bluffs.

As they came onto Goose Pond, Grange left them, heading for town with Charlie Chalk. Dan advised Walt to go back to Horse Creek, while he rode on with Hensa.

Dan dismounted and stepped up to the ranch house. He hesitated, then rapped at the door. Filena opened it, looked at the sheriff and moved away. Parker came from the dining-room, dabbing his mouth with a napkin. In the light from the porch lamps, he could see Hensa and the tilbury wagon, but he couldn't see the body of his son below the side boards.

Dan said, 'Let's go inside,' and he closed the door after him, attempting to draw the blow. He didn't know how to make a difference, so he did near enough what he did last time. 'It's Cotton, Mr Parker.'

Goose Parker had guessed most of it.

'Badly wounded?' he asked simply.

Dan shook his head. 'He's dead, Mr Parker.'

Parker's hand clutched the door frame. He dropped the napkin, and a low moan came from his lips. His shoulders sagged, but then he stiffened. He took a step towards the door, and Dan opened it. He pushed him to one side, and looked out at Hensa. 'Bring the boy in.'

Filena came to the corner of the front landing and stared at the wagon. Dan and Hensa carried Cotton's body into the house and laid him across a low sofa. Dan sensed Filena in the doorway looking at him, but he wasn't going to meet her eyes.

Parker asked, 'How did it happen?'

He told him fast, and straight. The best defence was attack, he could hide behind it. 'He'll never stand trial, Mr Parker, and that part of the evidence can be kept out.'

Half an hour after they'd ridden out, Dan turned to Hensa. He was thinking aloud.

'They're both responsible for his death. Someone got Cotton to do the dangerous work.'

They rode for another hour. 'There'll be an inquest in the morning. We'll need Walt.'

Grange was waiting for Dan when he reached town and together they walked into the River Bend Saloon. They looked like trouble. Even the saloon dog slunk off, tail between legs.

Ham Dorfmann was already there, and with Grange they covered the room. Dan walked straight across to Hayes's door, and knocked loudly. He took a step back. As the door swung open, Hayes stood framed in the backlight. He held a small ivory-handled gun close to his side. 'Well?' he asked dangerously.

Dan didn't make a move for his own gun. He stood motionless. 'You're under arrest.'

Hayes's eyes flicked from the sheriff, out to the saloon, but he made no move with his gun. It wasn't an option, having seen the look on Dan's face.

159

'What's the charge, Glass?'

'Conspiracy to murder, and I'll think of something else on the way over to the jail. And in the interests of your dignity, we'll forego the cuffs.'

'And who did I try to kill?'

'Give me the pretty gun, Carver. You won't be needing it.'

Dorfmann's voice boomed across the saloon. 'No. Stay where you are.'

The marshal had seen a movement from the barman, who was uncertain of his ground. He looked to Hayes for guidance, and the saloon owner smiled grimly. 'Find Thomas Feigh, and tell him I'll be needing bail.'

15

Run for the Border

The news of Carver Hayes's arrest spread fast. The respectable, and honest, citizens backed the sheriff, but the jury was crammed with friends of Feigh and Hayes. Even the prosecuting attorney was considered 'friendly' to the banker. Hayes attempted to get bail, but Judge Northwood gave nothing but the promise of a speedy trial.

There was also the news of Cotton Parker's death, and when the inquest was opened at Goose Pond the following morning, the men who rode alongside the cartel were there.

Dan told his story, and Walt, Hensa and Grange followed. In the midst of testimony,

Swinton Dobbs noisily claimed a verdict be brought against Walt. But Goose Parker helped the Horse Creek man in acquittal. He was mindful of Dan's assurance over his son's name.

When the crowd had left, Dan rode to Horse Creek to have a talk with his old friend, Hensa. With Lummock a deputy marshal, he knew it would be difficult to make an arrest, and when Will heard of Lummock's new office, he might take affairs into his own hands. Hayes's arrest might only be short-lived.

Hensa gave Dan his opinion. 'They're moving into a corner. Feigh's not going to sit idly by. Hayes'll get out somehow. The judge will have to set bail soon. If necessary they'll take it to Sedalia or Jefferson City. Once he's out, they'll string the case along for months.' He gave Dan a wily look. 'Perhaps Will's methods are best. Shoot their heads off.'

Dan thought it over as he rode back to

Eagle Spring. The late sun had slid away, and there was no sound other than his pony's hooves and its tetchy snort. He was drowsy, his chin bobbling against his chest, when a blow punched hard and sharp into the side of his head. He heard a distant crack as he slipped gently forward, trying to grip himself in the saddle. He toppled, smelling the acrid hide of his pony as his face crushed down its withers. The ground flashed pale, then very dark as it met his fall.

He swam up from the blackness, and the hurt and nausea hit him. He shivered, and raised a hand to his tacky, matted hair. He rolled onto his side, and vomited painfully. He groaned for a few minutes, then eased himself onto his knees. From somewhere near, a snort eddied through the air, and Dan whistled thinly. He heard the clink of his pony's heels as it moved in close, and he reached for a stirrup. He dragged himself up and into the saddle and, clutching the reins in one hand, and a hank of mane in the other, he asked the pony to move forward carefully.

On the slow meander to the outskirts of Eagle Spring, his head slowly cleared. His hat was gone, and the night air was refreshing against his forehead. By the time they reached the livery stable he was suffering a mere, dull, hammer-like pain.

He called out the doctor, and had his wound dressed. It was only a crease, but a close one. A little to the side, and the town would have been involved in another election.

Dan brushed aside Grange's questions and concern at his appearance. The deputy had to explain Hayes's release. 'They had an expensive lawyer up from Springfield, and he threatened a change of venue. It was a point of law apparently. Judge Northwood had to set bail.'

'What time was this ... that he got out?'

The deputy shrugged. 'I'm not certain. Early this afternoon.'

'Hard to believe, but it could account for

the bullet across my head.'

'You didn't see anything?'

Dan squeezed his eyelids together. 'No. I wasn't looking, was I? I was half asleep. The next thing I knew I was staring at the stars. Whoever it was, thought I was dead.'

The deputy nodded thoughtfully. 'There's talk that you're going before the jury in the morning. Giving evidence that's going to put Feigh away for a while.

Dan gave a half smile. 'Yeah. That's what I intended to do. I'm not so sure now.'

They had a meal at the hotel, then Dan decided to see if there was any reaction to the sight of him. They'd hardly set foot in the saloon when Carver Hayes arrived. He came straight at them, and if he was surprised at seeing Dan, he made good use of the professional poker face.

The gambler appeared puzzled. 'I'm sorry, Sheriff, but if you've been in any sort of trouble, and it looks as though you have, it's nothing to do with me. Nothing.'

'Is that right, Carver?' Dan's voice was

derisive. 'One day you'll have to tell me what is to do with you.'

A thin smile cracked Hayes's lips, but he didn't respond. He turned his back, and walked straight to his office door. He stopped before entering, and said something to Swinton Dobbs.

Grange said, 'He's very confident, Sheriff. Almost innocent.'

'It's not over yet, pard. Just wait and watch.'

In a few minutes, the office door opened, and Dobbs came out. He glanced at the sheriff and his deputy, and sneered. Grange muttered something unintelligible about gunmen, and stared at Dobbs's back.

They'd just drained their glasses when Walt rushed into the saloon. He made for Dan. 'Will's on the prod. When I told him Lummock was a marshal, he took off south. Someone's going to die again, Dan.'

The three men made a move to leave the saloon, but as they reached the doors, Thomas Feigh walked in. His face showed the expression that Dan had been seeking earlier from Hayes.

Feigh's mouth opened, even as he gargled, 'Sheriff.' Complicity, then surprise, dragged at his face. The banker was suddenly fearful, and for good reason. The evidence he was going to use to bludgeon his colleagues, had rebounded. Carver Hayes had heard tell, and Feigh had arrived to give an explanation.

Dan, Walt and Grange went straight to the sheriff's office, and Dan kicked the door shut. 'We've got to stop Will. How the hell do we do that? Walt?'

'I can't think of anyone who's up to that, Dan, except you. He's not going to reason it out. He'll find Lummock.'

Dan grimaced. 'Ride to Pittsburg, Walt. I'll go to Fort Scott. Lummock could be at either. Will's going to be close. If you find Lummock, dog him.'

Dan gathered the small packet from his desk, and went for Judge Northwood. Although Hensa said it would be a waste of time to present the evidence to a jury, Dan was determined.

He spent an hour with the judge, and the next morning he turned over the evidence to the jury. All he could do was wait. If the jury indicted the three men, it might be possible to prevent Will shooting Lummock.

There was no doubt about the hearing being a contentious and rowdy session. Voices were raised in fiery debate all day. Night descended on the town, and meals were brought from the hotel. Dan patrolled Main Street, or sat fiddling in the office. If his brother killed Lummock and came back, he'd have to do something. The fight on the timberline was a flea-bite in comparison. This was as personal as you could get. Two brothers.

Grange came in, and sat down. 'They're still arguing. You can almost hear them from here.'

Dan got up from his chair. He considered lashing out at something, but Ham Dorf-mann came bursting into the office.

'They're indicted,' he yelled at the sheriff and his deputy. 'All three of 'em.'

Dan found himself a hat. As he slapped it against his leg, the town marshal's face showed consternation. 'You going to arrest them?'

Dan eased the hat onto his head. 'No, not yet. They're not going anywhere that I can't get to them. I'm riding to Fort Scott. We'll arrest them when I get back. I've got to find Will, before he finds Lummock.'

In the night-time quiet, Goose Parker heard him arrive, and opened the door to meet him. The light spread from the main room, but Parker made no move to invite Dan inside. Dan told him the outcome of the hearing, then Filena stepped onto the stoop.

'And you'll be riding after Will then?' she asked with deadness in her voice.

Dan couldn't understand how anyone with so little obvious feeling for him, could look so attractive. 'You won't understand, will you, Filena? I'm trying to prevent another killing. Maybe his. And so far, he's actually innocent.'

He shook his head at her sadly, and thumped his spurs. He was gone too fast, and too soon, to see the liquid glister of her eyes. She grasped the hand of her father who stood silent in the doorway.

16

In and Out of Fort Scott

Not until the lights of Goose Pond had long faded from sight, was Dan aware of the sweat streaming from the pony's neck. He eased to a trot, slapping a hand against the wet silky hair. 'Miss Filena Parker's got right under my skin.'

On the second night, he tied his pony to a rail in front of the saloon at Fort Scott. The town was notorious along the border, and Dan knew that if Will had been seen, there'd be a man who would know where, and when.

Yellow smoke billowed through the huge drinking and gambling room. Dan's glance took in the clientele, as he walked slowly to the bar.

Two men he recognized as former employees of Carver Hayes, but there was no sign of Will, or Lummock. The bartender looked to Dan for his drink, but he shook his head. 'Not just now. Where's your boss?'

The bartender made a short movement with his hand, and almost in the same instant, Dan stood eye to eye with a massive, gold tie-pin.

The saloon owner bowed slightly to the sheriff. 'You wish to see me, sir? How can I help?' It wasn't just the man's six foot six that surprised Dan, but the snow white hair, and albino pink eyes.

'Is there somewhere we could talk? Somewhere a little more umm ... private?'

The saloon owner looked around him confidently, nodded, and led Dan to a small room.

Dan explained his problem, and the albino shook his head. 'I know nothing of your friend, sir, but I have seen the other man you refer to. Lummock did you say? He has been here recently. In this very saloon but a day or so ago. I am sorry. Perhaps I can offer you a drink?' He smiled openly.

It was sufficient for Dan. 'No. No, thank you. You've been helpful.'

The man had no reason to lie. But thinking this, Dan failed to catch the deceitful charm that flicked across the pale, rose-coloured eyes. He nodded his appreciation, and made for the door. If Lummock was a day, or even more, ahead of him, it was hopeless. He would have to take a chance on Walt catching up with his brother.

Within an hour he was heading north. Back to Eagle Spring, where two men were ready to savour the law.

For a while after Dan had gone, the saloon owner sat contemplating a fistful of gold and silver rings. He eventually got up and opened a door that led to another, but more private and darker, room.

Almost immediately, Pole Lummock appeared, and he laughed loudly.

'Well done, Ivory.'

The albino shrugged. 'You and your friends are in deep trouble, believe me.'

Lummock's laugh continued. 'Feigh and Hayes, both indicted. That really is too bad. I always had a feeling about the banker. He's not an honest man ... ha ha. But now I'm a US deputy marshal, with the full backing of the law, they can't touch me.'

The saloon owner raised his head, and squinted at Lummock. 'If the man who's just left here is the man you're up against, and as I understand he has a "friend", you'll need a lot more than the full backing of the law.'

Some time later, the one-time sheriff of Eagle Spring elbowed his way through the crowded saloon and into the street. He was after an advantage, and didn't know, or care, for the whereabouts of Will Glass. The warning of Ivory was clouded by approaching megalomania. He saw no reason why he couldn't return to Eagle Spring. Once upon the buckboard, he'd be difficult to get down. Dan Glass would be forced to safeguard him. The fantasy was so pleasurable that he failed to see or hear the rider who'd followed him out of town, and back into Missouri.

It was two in the morning when Lummock neared a line shack of Goose Pond. It was unoccupied, and he decided to spend the rest of the night there. He had intended to meet with his new boss in Fort Scott, but the man was an old-timer, and would know to follow him to Eagle Spring.

As dawn streaked across the Breaks, Lummock stretched, and looked around the line shack's staple supplies. He walked outside with a hot cup of coffee, when a quiet voice surprised him. The tin mug fell from his fingers, spilling down his front, and across his boots.

Will was unmoving, hands at his sides and very unsmiling. His voice was flat and detached, and it drained life from the marshal's face. 'Pole Lummock, Deputy US Marshal out of Fort Scott, died today.'

Lummock was unarmed, and he glanced

at the open door of the shack. But Will spoke again. 'Talk to me, before you die, Lummock.'

'You're going to kill me? That will be murder, this time.'

'Tell me who killed my father, then I'll kill you. But it won't be murder.'

Will stepped into the cabin. In a moment he reappeared with another tin mug, and the marshal's gunbelt over his shoulder. He hunkered at the coffee pot, and laid the gun and belt at his feet. While he poured coffee, his eyes never moved from Lummock's face.

Lummock swayed backwards with an almost imperceptible movement. 'I wasn't after you. I've been indicted with Thomas Feigh and Carver Hayes. I'm going back to give myself up.'

A cruel twitch moved in Will's face. He tossed Lummock his gunbelt. 'Put it on, and tell me about my father.'

Lummock tried again. 'Cotton Parker hired Moss Trinkett, and that's the God's honest truth. You already killed Trinkett, and your man, Walt, blew Parker apart.'

'One of the bullets was from a Sharps. *Your* Sharps, Lummock. The one there in the shack.' Will moved his coat away from his left-hand side, revealing one of his father's .44 Smith & Wessons.

Lummock knew that time had run out, and he leaned to fasten the holster strap to his leg. Then he flung himself aside, drawing at his Colt. With his finger on the trigger, he jerked back the hammer twice in rapid succession. As he hit the ground heavily, he was watching Will Glass. But then there was confusion, and he involuntarily doubled from the waist. He rolled into a ball, and grinned his last grin as he tasted the blood. He tried to keep his eyes open, but they clouded. He said the words, but he was curiously worried that Will wouldn't hear them. 'I'll see you down there, *boy.*'

Will gripped his coat against the bullet wound in his side. 'One day, Lummock. One day.' He whistled for his pony, and still clutching the revolver, he climbed wearily into the saddle.

He sat on his pony and, looking down at Lummock's body, he thought for a few seconds. 'Maybe Dan can handle the rest of 'em. Trinkett, Church, Cotton Parker and now Lummock. Four-for-one, so far, Dad.'

It was intuition that made Will suddenly duck forward. A bullet slapped and whined off broken shale, and he heard the accompanying rifle shot. He kicked at the pony's flanks with his spurs as another bullet ricocheted close too. He bent low over the animal's neck, and with a scornful yell galloped east.

17

The Lynching Party

Dan reached Eagle Spring in the early morning, but it was mid-afternoon before Grange's voice woke him. Walt was also in the office when he came out. He asked Dan, 'Did you find Will?'

Dan yawned, and shook his head. 'I don't think he'd been seen for weeks.'

Walt looked thwarted. 'I couldn't find out much either. Nobody's seen them. Maybe they're playing tag along the timberline?'

Dan turned to his deputy. 'Get hold of Dorfmann. We'll get those warrants out.'

Grange looked sheepishly at Dan. 'Can't do, Sheriff, and waking you up wouldn't have helped. Feigh and Hayes gave themselves up. They had a highrollin' lawyer.

There's no charges being brought. Judge Twitchell quashed it on a technicality.'

Dan's fists clenched in anger. 'What technicality?'

Grange shrugged. 'The judge'll explain. Spelled someone's name wrong, or something. Damned if I know. An' now they're free, and there's big trouble brewing.'

Dan said grimly, 'What else?'

'Well, Feigh and Hayes are pretty mad at each other, and Feigh's closing down on all the north spreads that owe money. Judge Northwood says it's legal.' Grange looked as though he didn't want to go on, as if he was partly to blame in the sheriff's absence. 'They'll form a lynch party, Dan. Feigh knows it, and he's scared to death. He's asked Carver Hayes to loan him a couple of men with guns, but he got the bum's rush.'

Dan was furious at the legal chicanery, and hurried to see Judge Northwood for an explanation.

'I know how you feel, Sheriff. It is a travesty to let those two go free. Sometimes justice and law are different animals. They could go to a supreme court.'

'But these loan foreclosures from the bank, from Thomas Feigh. Are they legal?'

The judge nodded glumly. 'Wholly. If any of the ranchers had employed an attorney, they'd have known.'

'Attorney? Who the hell ever hired an attorney out here? They were encouraged to borrow money, and in good faith.'

The judge looked ruefully at Dan. 'I know that, but it doesn't help.'

Dan went straight to the home of the banker. Feigh was relieved to see him. 'You'll give me protection, Sheriff?' he asked anxiously.

'I guess I'll have to, Mr Feigh. At the moment I'm legally obliged to protect the corruption you stand for.'

The banker was so distressed that the slander appeared to have little or no effect. Dan went back to his office, and told Grange and Ham Dorfmann to arrange the banker's protection. He then got a horse from the livery stable, and rode north, hoping to stamp on any trouble before it reached town.

His first call was at the ranch of a dogged Tommy Dinner.

'We ain't waiting for the law this time, Sheriff. Don't get in the way. We need a turkey to make a new thanksgiving.'

As he turned away, Dan shouted to the old rancher, 'You didn't wait for the law last time, Tommy.'

Hector Redwing's anger was just as great. Argument was just as useless, and Dan couldn't really blame them. He was the appointed sheriff though, and they'd only get to Feigh through his badge.

Dan didn't waste any time in the search for deputies. The few hands that were available, weren't having anything to do with protecting Thomas Feigh. As a last resort, he tried Carver Hayes. He'd been an accomplice of Feigh, and Dan couldn't believe the saloon owner would allow the underdogs to form a vigilante group.

Hayes was sarcastically friendly as Dan followed him into his office. 'So you'd like to raise a guard for Thomas Feigh? That's rich, Sheriff. No luck elsewhere, I'd guess.'

Dan nodded. 'I'm here as a last resort. I've got no one, except my deputy and Dorfmann.'

Hayes winked at the sheriff. 'And that's the way it's going to stay.'

Dan sat down in Hayes's comfortable chair, and slowly rolled himself a cigarette. 'Let's look at this another way, Carver. You don't know what was stolen from Feigh. But you know he'll blab in a few hours' time if a lynch mob gets to him. How he'll lay everything at someone else's door, in order to save his own fat neck. You see, I know what he kept in his diary. Your name's there. It's incriminating.'

Hayes's face twitched. 'Go on, Sheriff, I'm listening.'

Dan smiled. 'This is the way I see it. Feigh's played both ends against the middle.

He's like that. He doesn't care for you, or gamblers in general, and he's no use for Lummock, or Cotton Parker. Think about it. He'll go down squawking.'

Hayes showed Dan to the office door. 'I'll get together a few men. I might even be there myself.'

After collecting ammunition and a rifle, Dan went to see the banker again. Alex let him in, and Dan told them what he'd arranged. He guessed Mrs Feigh was still in safe hiding.

Feigh was clearly frightened. 'Good God, Sheriff, Hayes will kill me.'

Dan shook his head. 'That's what you're supposed to think, Mr Feigh. But you're worth a lot more alive.'

Fingers rapped at the front door, and before Dan could stop her, Alex opened it. He stood behind her, his hand on his gun. It was Hayes. He took off his hat to the girl, and Dan followed him through into the study.

Hayes said, 'Good evening, Tom. I

suppose the sheriff has told you I've brought men to protect you?'

There was sudden shouting from the street, and Dan stepped out to the porch. Carver Hayes's motley collection, the bartender, croupier and four others were stationed around the house. Dan saw Grange talking to someone across the street, and Dorfmann was close beside him. With the man between them, they approached the house. The man was Hector Redwing.

Dan said, 'Well, what's it going to be this time, Hector?'

Redwing was still angered. 'I've nearly twenty men here, Sheriff, and I don't want anyone to get hurt. You and the girl, please get out of the way. It's the banker we want.'

Dan smiled coldly. 'You'll have to do a lot better than that. Hayes's men are here. I think you should go home.'

Redwing looked slightly dismayed. 'Carver's men are here? Where are they?'

Dan looked around him. 'They're here. If you want to see them, Lem'll introduce you.

You can't take the law into your own hands, Hector. Haven't you learnt anything?' He leant in closer to Redwing. 'Besides, I'll tell three of four of them to shoot *you* first. How about that, for a reason to go home?'

The rancher knew the sheriff wasn't bluffing, and backed into the street. He had a knowing word with his men, and in a few minutes came back. 'We're listening, Sheriff. He's not worth spilling blood over.'

Dan looked at him, and silently mouthed the word, *'yours'*.

The rancher hadn't quite finished. 'Get him to cancel the foreclosures. You tell him that's what we want.'

'Thanks, Hector. I'll tell him.'

When the erstwhile lynch party had vanished from town, Hayes sent his men back to the saloon. Dan saw his deputy and the marshal off on a round of the town.

Alex Feigh stopped him. 'Sheriff,' she said huskily. 'I'd like to go for a ride. Somewhere away from here.'

He grinned, loving the voice. 'How many

guns will I need?'

The girl turned her head away, but her eyes were smiling.

He got a buggy from the livery stable, and they trotted east, to where the bluffs overlooked an arroyo of the Piney.

Alex looked quickly up at the sky, then down at her clasped hands.

'I hate it here now, in Eagle Spring.'

The texture of her voice disguised the bitterness, but it was there, and it startled him.

'I think you know why. It's my father ... those men.'

Dan was surprised. 'Are you saying you don't know what your father's doing? What he's involved in?'

'He tells me nothing. Not even my mother. But you know, don't you?'

Dan believed her, and he could only guess at why she didn't know. Was her father trying to protect *her*, or simply protecting his *own* standing? He told her what he knew. Some of it was well known, but some of it wasn't. Some of it, he bent gently.

187

'That's about the long and the short of it, Alex. Will's still out there, and if I can't stop him, he'll have a crack at your father.'

It was getting late when they returned to the Feigh home. As Alex turned to get down from the buggy, a man came running from the house to meet them. It was one of the banker's clerks.

'We've been looking ... for you, Miss ... and you, Sheriff.' The man's voice was faltering with emotion.

Dan vaulted to the ground. 'What's going on? What's happened?'

The man spluttered, 'It's Mr Feigh. He's been shot ... dead.'

Dan reached out and took hold of Alex as she slid from the buggy. He helped her into the house, and then saw the body of her father. Through a half-open door into another room, he caught sight of Feigh's wife sitting in a chair. She was staring out at him, but there was no sign of recognition or understanding.

From the clerk, he got as much of the story as he could.

Feigh and Hayes had been talking quietly, then there were raised voices. Hayes started swearing, then shouting at Feigh. Then the banker threatened Hayes. Then the gunshot.

18

The Trail of Carver Hayes

Dan saw the change in Alex. It was later, when she'd taken care of her father. There was grief in her face, but also something else. Something unsettled.

'You'll find him, and bring him back?' She looked at him as if she wasn't sure he'd try.

He gripped her hand, and smiled grimly. 'I'll get him. I promise.'

This time it was easier to form a posse. There were now plenty of men willing to go after Hayes. Dan gave them a quick briefing, then went to the River Bend Saloon. The bartender looked at him with open suspicion when he asked the whereabouts of Hayes. Dan's persuasive approach was fruitless. The bartender didn't know anything.

It was Kitty Liddle, from the hotel, who gave him the information he needed. It wasn't much, but she wanted to help. 'I saw him ride out. He went east, towards the foothills.'

Within an hour, the posse had mounted, and Grange had hired a Cheyenne to help on the trail. Several times the posse stopped while Fat Tail dismounted to put his ear to the ground, or inspect signs.

They'd reached the Ozarks, before the Indian spoke for the first time.

'Rider not going south any more.' He pointed up to the high, sharp ridges. 'Two narrow canyons through the peaks.' He held up two fingers side by side. 'We go there.'

Fat Tail pulled up his horse's head, and looked to Dan and Grange.

Grange looked questioningly at Dan. 'What do you think?'

Dan was uncertain, 'I don't. He's the one doing the tracking. Maybe Hayes is going to Pittsburg.' He nodded once, quickly at the Indian.

They followed Fat Tail up through ridges and gullies, climbing ever higher through the timberline. There was only a sliver of moon when the Indian eventually slid from his horse, and held up his hand.

Fat Tail and the rest of the posse were positioned along the top of the ridge, where they could cover the narrow canyon from every angle. If Hayes was there, Dan would try and make escape impossible. One of the posse led the horses to picket, down and away from the ridge.

On the canyon floor, a speck of light flared and then died, and a horse snorted uneasily. The flames grew again into an orange glow, then rose higher, as the camp-fire took hold.

Dan watched as the fire leaped, curiously spreading into the darkness of the canyon floor. 'Whoever that is down there's doing a bit more than spitting a rabbit.'

He'd no sooner spoken to Grange, than the crack of a revolver slammed around the walls of the canyon. Then another. Then more, as bullet after bullet crashed and whined around them. Dan was staring hard at the fire, but in the spreading glow, he could see no sign of movement other than the blossoming flames. There *weren't* any men down in the canyon firing guns.

As he watched the stretching flames, he knew the reason. Carver Hayes, and whoever he was with, knew about the posse. They'd fired the canyon to drive the sheriff and his men back over the ridge, trapping them, turning the tables.

A lance of yellow flame scrambled into a dry pine, spitting needles of flaming resin high into the black sky. The scrub-sided gully was rolling upwards, ablaze with orange and crimson, and moon-coloured smoke.

Dan stared around him, cursing for believing, then following, the Indian. He looked for his deputy, but couldn't see him. Already the smoke was curling over the ridge, filling their lungs and stinging their eyes. He called to the men around him, shouting over the intense crackle of the advancing fire. 'Leave Hayes. Get moving. Back off to the ridge.'

He watched as several of his men ran from hiding, stumbling, fearful and awkward down the shaled sides of the ridge. The heated air in the gully was driving the fire up to the canyon crest, then over. The flames were momentarily held, but Dan was afraid they wouldn't reach the horses before becoming engulfed in the blaze.

Grange suddenly appeared out of the smoky darkness, silhouetted against the crimson glow. 'We'll never make it. There's four of 'em on the far ridge.' He nodded towards the gully where the horses were picketed. 'When the fire's right behind us, they'll have a turkey shoot. I shot the Indian. His fat tail's got two holes in it now.' He laughed grimly.

Three other men showed themselves, and Dan said quickly, 'There's only the one way out, back over that ridge. Maybe there's four of them, but there's five of us. We've got to get the horses back up there, before the fire reaches us. Let's go.'

Dan, Lem Grange, and the rest of the posse scrambled down the rocky slope. Ahead, and above them, the flash and crash of bullets let them know they'd been seen. In a wild and angry reprisal, Dan loosed off two shots into the ridge. From alongside him, his men poured steady gunfire at the four men hidden above them. To the right, a ranch hand yelled, and went crashing to the ground. Dan pulled him to his feet, and with one hand gripped tight around the man's gunbelt, he continued down towards the horses.

Above them a scream pierced the crash of the posse's guns and the roaring fire. A body fell from the top of the ridge and landed lifeless on the gully floor. Someone had made a lucky hit, and Dan wondered if that left only three. He stumbled on down to the frightened horses that were stamping and whinnying into the hot, thick air. He let go the rancher, and the injured body crumpled at his feet.

A figure came charging out from the darkness. Dan fired another two shots into the man's midriff, and the man pitched forward onto his face. His outstretched arms flailed at the horse's hooves, inciting them to even greater alarm.

Behind them, and almost overhead, the sky was a rampant, bloody glow. The fire was eating down from the ridge-top, sweeping out of the first gully, down into the second. The men were covered in fine ash, and exhausted.

Dan's voice grated at his deputy. 'There's no firing. What's happened to the others? Where's Hayes?'

Grange's face was shiny, and black with sweat and soot. 'There was four, Dan. Two of 'em have run, and Hayes is one of 'em.'

Grange, and one of the other men, carried the wounded ranch hand to his horse. Within minutes they were all mounted and, with Grange leading, and Dan following on, they crossed the gully. Away from the advancing flames, the animals calmed, and responded to their riders. As they trailed back from the timberline slopes to the flat rangeland, more riders joined them. They were the rest of the posse from the far side of the canyon.

They left the wounded ranch hand at Doc Heggarty's, back in Eagle Spring. It wasn't a serious injury. A rifle bullet had sliced across the back of his shoulders, and he was weak from shock, and loss of blood.

Dorfmann was waiting at the sheriff's office, and Dan explained what had happened. He looked dubiously at the marshal.

'Ham, there's just a bit more before we're finished. With you and Lem, I've something to work on. Hayes is up for a hangin' now, but he must think we're badly hit. I bet he'll come back to the River Bend. Wherever he tries to get to, he'll need money.'

Grange and Dorfmann looked at each other, then at Dan. Dorfmann nodded, and Grange spoke for both of them. 'Yeah. We'll come with you.'

The three men walked up the street to Carver Hayes's River Bend Saloon. Dan pushed through the swing doors, and the deputy and town marshal followed closely. It was late, but there were still men drinking and gambling at the tables. A few of them lolled at the bar, and the dog made its way to a safer hiding place.

Dorfmann and Grange stood either side of the doors. Dan's way was barred by Swinton Dobbs.

'There's nobody in, Sheriff. Nobody except me, and I've taken over.'

Dan gave the man a slight, wry smile. Then he squeezed his fist, and swung a ridge of knuckles into the side of Dobbs's jaw. The gunman's head jerked from the blow, and he sprawled backward. He crashed into a table, and it collapsed under him amidst a shower of glass and playing cards. Dan waited for Dobbs to claw at his gun. Then he ground his heel into the back of the man's hand, and kicked the gun from his rigid fingers.

At the same time, Grange took one step forward, and roared into the saloon, 'Leave the gun.'

The bartender had brought up a scattergun from under the bar. He'd started to turn it towards Dan, but Grange fired. The scattergun exploded, a blur of shot tearing into the ceiling above Dan and Swinton Dobbs. The barman slammed against the rear of the bar, then moved forward slightly, his face crushing into a pool of booze across the counter top.

If any of the remaining customers had any thoughts of making a backing move, the destruction of the bartender made them think twice.

Dorfmann yelled at them, 'Empty your belts here. Put your guns on the table before you leave. Now.'

The only one who attempted to protest was Dobbs. He snarled, 'Hayes'll get to you, Glass, if I don't.'

Dan almost admired the man's character, but he shook his head. 'A sense of humour,

Dobbs, try and keep it.'

With the barrel of his gun pushing hard into the flesh of Dobbs's neck, he goaded the gunman across the floor of the saloon and out onto the sidewalk. 'Don't ever come back, Dobbs. Next time I'll pull the trigger.'

He called to Grange and Dorfmann, and pointed to Hayes's office. 'Watch the door.'

He stood to one side, out of the line of fire if Hayes shot through it. He tried the knob, but the door was locked. He called, 'Come on, Hayes, it's all over. Everyone's dead or gone.'

A great double-blast took out the whole centre section of the door. It splintered into the back of the bar, peppering and shifting the crumpled body of the dead barman. It was Hayes with a shotgun. Dan knew the office, there was no other way of getting out of the building. Hayes would have to come through the door.

In the thick silence that followed, Dan made no sound, other than a calculated groan, then he threw himself loudly to the floor. The remains of the door were kicked open, and Hayes burst through. He was swinging up the barrels of his shotgun after reloading, but he'd got it wrong. Dan was lying in front of him almost at his feet.

Grange was firing, but it was Ham Dorfmann who caught the blast from Hayes's gun, and he fell sideways under the impact. Hayes's eyes flashed, and Dan watched, fascinated, as the man steadied himself to raise the shotgun once again. He levelled the barrel down at Dan.

Dan said quietly, 'No, Hayes,' and fired his Smith & Wesson. The second shot from Hayes's gun tore into the floor, catching Dan's upper legs, and he grunted as the pain seared.

Hayes was dying. His eyes rolled, then closed, as he crumpled down and across Dan's legs. Dan pushed out, rolling the body desperately away from the pain. His head fell back, and he lay facing the ceiling. His breath came in thin, wearied gasps, before the heavy curtain of sleep.

19

The Glass Brothers

The sheriff was swimming into consciousness. There were two people, and, as his eyes cleared, he was aware of Filena Parker gripping his hand. He saw the smile that crossed her face. 'Hello Filena, Doc. I'm alive then?'

Doc Heggarty looked at Dan, and said, without much expression, 'Yes, you are. Your legs are a bit of a mess, but everything else is OK. Shame the pellets didn't catch you in the head. You'd have been all right then.' The doctor picked up his bag. 'And in case you're interested, Hayes is dead and his barman. Your opponents don't do well in this town.'

Dan could still see the look in Hayes's eyes as he swung his shotgun, and he shivered as

Heggarty left the room.

'This is the first time I've held your hand, since we were in school. The picnic at Bear Lake.'

Filena was doubtful. 'You never held my hand in school.'

Dan puffed a thin column of air, then twisted towards her. The pain made him wince. 'Aagh, my legs hurt. Even when I talk.'

Filena looked amused. 'Well, don't.'

'It's a shame, isn't it? All I ever do, is bring you grief.'

She gave him the look he'd seen in the hotel. He thought she really was the most beautiful girl he'd ever seen. 'The grief's finished now. It has to be. Everyone's enemies are dead.'

Dan was confused. 'No, there's still Lummock ... isn't there?'

'I thought you knew. He was shot, out at our line shack.'

'Who?' The sheriff's voice was getting thin and strained.

Filena shook her head. 'Nobody seems to know. Charlie found his body when he took a new cow hand out there. He'd been dead for a few days.'

'Why didn't someone tell me?'

Filena laughed gently. 'How was *someone,* supposed to do that? You couldn't have done much about it. You'll be in bed for a week. Deputy Grange is going to look after the town for a while.'

The doctor and Filena conspired to keep him in bed for three days, but he grew restless. He wanted up, and his wounds weren't that bad once the pain had gone. He needed to find out about Lummock.

He managed to climb on a horse, and with Grange and Charlie Chalk, he rode out to the line shack. By that time, Lummock had been buried, but his saddle, gunbelt and Sharps carbine had been left for Dan to see. Dan saw that two shots had been fired from Lummock's gun. That meant that he'd put up a fight, had a chance. There was nothing to link Will with his death.

When Glass and Grange returned to town, Dorfmann met them in the middle of the street, and he wasn't waiting for Dan to dismount. 'Will's shot and killed Lummock. There's a Marshal Stone here. He's waiting for you in the office.'

Dan winced. It was what he'd been dreading. He recalled Walt's words: *'Someone's going to die again, Dan.'*

Dorfmann was running off parts of the story. 'Stone saw it all, Dan. He's got Will pegged out with this one. Stone wasn't more 'an a half-mile away, and he recognized Lummock's horse. That grey. As big and slow as a rain cloud. Two or three shots ... they was that close together.'

Dan heard the marshal, but he was barely listening. He climbed stiffly from his horse, and handed the reins to Dorfmann.

A tall, ageing man got up slowly from his chair to greet him as he entered his office. 'Howdy, Sheriff,' he said with a friendly smile. 'I'm Rufus Stone, and I brought you bad news.'

Dan extended his hand. 'Marshal. I hope you're not as pleased as you sound.' He looked at the bandanna wrapped around Stone's fist.

'I took a bullet from your *friend*,' Stone explained. 'But I'll tell you the whole story. You'll need to know, before you go after him.'

Dan's eyes would have given him away, but his face didn't change. As Stone went on with his story, Dan grabbed a bottle of whiskey from his desk drawer, and placed a couple of glasses between them. He asked, 'What happened after you shot him?'

The marshal sighed, and looked wearily at his glass. 'I trailed him, most of that day, and into the night. I was very tired. I'd wasted a lot of time looking for Lummock. I dug in for a while, on the other side of the Ozarks. I had a good long sleep, and the sun was right up when I woke. I was probably making a lot of noise, and there he was all of a sudden, on the paint, just smiling.'

Stone swilled the last of his whiskey. 'Took

me by surprise. Happens a lot nowadays. I went for my gun, and it was all he needed. He was very quick.' Stone looked rueful and lifted his injured hand. 'He asked me if I was trailing him. I told him I was, that I was taking him in for killing Pole Lummock. He laughed 'til he was fit to bust. He never took his eyes off me though, I remember that. Then he asked me how I aimed to do it, take him in, that is. He gave me his bandanna. Then, before he rode off, he told me that I'd meet his brother in Eagle Spring. And that I was to tell him, that he was riding for the border, maybe clear to Kansas City.'

Dan looked straight at the marshal. 'And now you want *me* to bring him in.'

Stone nodded. 'You're the sheriff, and it wasn't more'n twenty-four hours ago. I'll deputize you as a US marshal to go get him. Here's a badge. A mite battered, but it'll serve.'

Dan took the star, and looked at it questioningly. He flipped it onto the desk top. 'I don't need this. If I bring my brother in, give me your word he'll get a fair trial.'

'You've got it,' Stone said, and got to his feet. 'You bring your brother in, and I'll back you. There'll be no lynch party.'

After Stone had gone, Dan sat for a long time on his own, thinking. Eventually he grabbed his hat and gunbelt, then slumped from his office. There was someone he wanted to see before he took off after Will.

Filena could see the torment written across his face. Dan told her what Marshal Stone had said, and what was expected of him.

'You don't always do everything you're told to, do you?'

He looked at the ground. 'I'm either the sheriff, or I'm not. In the same way as I'm Dan Glass, or not. There's not much difference.'

Filena shook her head. 'He'll be out of the state in a few days. You won't be catching him anyway, so let him keep the advantage.'

Dan stood up. There was his conscience,

like a hangover. 'I can't. I'm sorry. Will knows that.'

'I hope for your sake he does, Daniel Glass. I truly hope he does.' Turning her back, she flounced from the room.

Dan was back to square one again. He ground his teeth, slammed the door loudly and rudely behind him, and spurred his pony back to town.

Ham Dorfmann saw him later, stuffing meats and coffee into his saddle-bags. He'd got a horse, the best one in the corral. It was a big bay, made for a rough ride.

Dorfmann tried to argue him out of the trip. 'The county's cleaning up good now, Dan. Miss Alex's giving all them ranchers time. She ain't a bit like her old man.' He patted the horse on its muscly rump. 'Let Marshal Stone bring him in.'

The sheriff was exasperated with explaining. 'It's part of my job, Ham, you know it. Everybody knows it.'

Dorfmann did know it, but was more frustrated. 'Well, if I had a brother – I want no part of it. I'm resigning.' He turned away sadly, and tracked off down the street.

A short time later, Dan hoisted himself onto the bay. No one spoke to him as he cantered out of town, but some of Lummock's friends muttered amongst themselves.

One of the older ranchers said to a colleague, 'Wonder if that's the last we've seen of our sheriff? You wouldn't catch me going up against Will Glass. Brother or not.'

The colleague stabbed a finger against the old man's chest. 'You should be supporting him. We all should. He's the first sheriff we've had who ain't crooked. He's a good man, who don't side. And I'll tell you this: I don't believe his brother's guilty, an' if it came to a fight, I wouldn't like to live on the difference between the pair of 'em.'

Dan crossed the northern half of Goose Pond, then through the pass to Horse Creek flats. He then swung south-west, to the climbing trail of the Ozarks. He knew exactly where Stone had been confronted by Will. It was where the brothers had play-hunted as children. He reckoned that Will wouldn't have feed for a long ride. He'd probably camp for a day or two, until he'd got meats. There was rabbit, bird and wild onion in the gullies.

The peaks were tinged by the late sun when Dan slipped quietly from his horse. He hitched him up, and walked cautiously through the pines. He no longer felt disturbed, it was something he had to get on with. If he brought Will in, he'd be a pariah. Filena had turned against him, two or three times. And now Ham Dorfmann.

He crawled over the dense matting of pine needles, making his way toward the coop that he and Will had built as kids. He started to hope he was wrong, that Will wouldn't be there. He wasn't convinced by Stone's reading of what had happened. It didn't have the tang of murder. An execution, maybe.

His nerves tingled when he saw a boot poking out from the old, wicker shelter. He bunkered behind the bole of a big pine, his

Winchester pointing skywards. 'Will? We've got to talk.... You're in big trouble. Come out. Will?'

Will rolled sideways out of the coop, and Dan yelled for his brother to leave his gun. But Will recognized the voice. He tucked his revolver into his pants top, shook himself out of his blanket and stumbled to his feet.

'Drop your gun, Will ... please.'

Will smiled. 'Yeah, Dan.' He carefully dropped his revolver to the ground. 'Dan? What's going on?'

Dan walked towards his brother and picked up his gun. It was the Smith & Wesson that matched his own. He didn't say anything, just watched. Will started to rekindle the small fire. 'What's happened in town, Dan?'

Dan shrugged away the wonder of Will's guile, and began to tell him what had happened. He looked carefully at his brother. 'Stone said there'd be a fair trial, Will.'

Will shrugged. He stared at his gun in

Dan's hand. 'Lummock fired twice before I hit him. He had his chance. It was more than he gave old Malachy, Dan ... our dad.'

'I believe you, Will, and there's no reason for you not to come in with me. You're being as stubborn, as I am pompous. Horse Creek's still waiting. We've done what we set out to do.'

'Maybe,' Will answered.

When the pony had been saddled, Dan led them to his own mount.

Will said, 'Maybe you'd better slip the cuffs on me.' He laughed loudly. 'Pompous, eh? Where did that come from?'

Dan looked at his brother and smiled. 'Filena Parker.'

He handed Will back his gunbelt. 'Let me know what Kansas City's like.' Then he swung the bay's head away, and broke into a sharp gallop, up and back to the eastern side of the timberline.

20

Gun Law

Dan had gone beyond the timberline, still climbing. He was contemplating the long drift back to Eagle Spring. Ahead, and to one side of him, the thinning pines couldn't quite conceal the coat of his brother's pony. It was one of their 'little-guy' rules. If you couldn't see the rider, then it didn't count. He smiled wistfully.

Will backed his pony into Dan's path. 'I didn't say I wasn't coming with you.'

Dan shook his head. 'Tell me, Will: Why have I gone to all this trouble? Why didn't I let Stone do it?'

Will raised his eyebrows. 'Because you knew he couldn't.' He handed over his gunbelt. 'You can't bring in an outlaw who's still wearing his guns. Anyway, I've thought it over. I'll stand trial. Perhaps Lummock's friends *will* arrange a necktie party. Just think on that, Brother. What a gunfight you'll have.'

The day's heat had changed to twilight chill as the sheriff and his prisoner jostled into Eagle Spring. They stopped outside the jail, and climbed awkwardly from their ponies. They walked in and found Ham Dorfmann, dozing in his chair. As Dan kicked the door shut, Ham jumped to his feet. He made a wild grab for his gun, but Dan held up his hands.

'Take it easy.'

Will laughed. 'Pleased to see me, Ham? Nice-looking offices.' He eyed the bars of a cell. 'Not so bad. First time I've seen the inside.' He winked at the town marshal. 'Keep a beady eye on me.' He put two fingers of his left hand together, and pistol-pointed them at the marshal. He made a kid's shooting noise in his mouth, and Dorfmann smiled, embarrassed.

The marshal looked at Dan. 'Which of these cells do you want me to put him in?'

'The best one.'

'There isn't a best one.'

Dan had begun to feel the guilt. He could have left Will alone, and he'd be heading out of the state by now. 'Pompous *and* pig-headed' Dorfmann's question rubbed him a bit rawer.

'Just put him in a cell.'

Will nudged Dorfmann as they walked into the barred cell. 'Don't know why he's so umpty. He's beat me at hands-up, and hide an' seek.'

Dorfmann still looked miserable. 'You shouldn't have come in. It'll take more than US Marshal Stone to keep the Hayes and Lummock mob down. They've been swaggering the street all day, telling anyone who'll listen that there's going to be a hanging.'

Dorfmann stepped back into the front office. Dan was sitting at his desk, with his head buried in his arms. The town marshal put his huge hand around Dan's shoulder and gripped it. 'I haven't really resigned, Dan. I can't, can I? Got to uphold the law you're always going on about. I'm thinking you'll be needing an extra gun.'

Dan looked up. 'Thanks, Ham. Will you order some dinner from the hotel for me and Will? And tell Stone that the outlaw's here in jail.'

Outside in the street, men gathered in little groups. Some had started to make wagers on the outcome; others left town on secret assignations. Marshal Stone's account of Lummock's death had made things worse for Will Glass. Swinton Dobbs, now seemingly running the saloon, had helped with lurid tales of ruthless behaviour.

Dobbs was an eel, who thought he could slick into Hayes's shoes and carry on the business of the cartel. But Dan temporarily closed the saloon, pending a decision on all Hayes's property and possessions.

Kitty Liddle brought the Glass brothers

their dinner. She wanted to hear the story of Will's capture, but Dan thanked her for the food, and politely showed her the door. He unlocked the cell and Will stepped out to sit with him at the desk in the front office.

As they ate, the brothers discussed the possibility of making a stand at the jail. When they'd finished, Rufus Stone arrived with Grange, and Will greeted him without animosity.

'Howdy-do, Marshal. I hope you're not seeking revenge for me shooting up your gun hand. I'm right sorry about it.'

Stone grinned. 'It was good shooting, Glass. And it's not so bad, as it turns out. I've been considering retiring, turning in the badge. Suppose you tell me the details of what happened out there at the line shack. You'll be surprised to hear that I was never that close to Pole Lummock.'

Will told Stone all he could think of, or remember. When he told him of the shooting, the US marshal's demeanour was less cold.

The marshal turned to Dan. 'What you got in mind, Sheriff? When do you expect them? We have to stay alive, if this becomes a shooting gallery.'

'Dobbs has opened the saloon again, and they're climbing the walls. When they're all drunk enough, they'll come.'

Dorfmann made towards the small storeroom. 'I visited the store this afternoon and took most of the ammunition. We've enough rifles and handguns. We can give a good account of ourselves if we have to, if that's what they're after.'

Grange said, 'Oh, that's what they're after, Ham. I'll walk the street. They won't start anything yet. If they do, you can let me in the back door.'

Dan agreed, and Grange left the jail. Dorfmann looked bitterly at Stone. 'If you'd have kept your mouth shut, all this might have turned out a bit different.'

Stone smiled resignedly. 'It wouldn't have made any difference, and you know it.'

It was quiet for a few moments, then Dan

said, 'Will, I'm damned sorry I brought you back to this. Stone gave me a promise that he can't keep.' He looked openly at his brother. 'There's a back door. Your pony's in the corral, and there's other horses. You can get out now. We can't hold them all off.' He looked to Stone for his reaction.

The marshal nodded his head in agreement. 'Your brother's right, go on. Life's too short. Anyway, I haven't had time to get a warrant. For the record, Deputy Marshal Lummock was killed while on duty. There's no clues, or evidence that points to you.'

Will knew it was difficult for the two lawmen to make the decision. They were compromising themselves, and the law. But it was the only practical answer. If he was going to die, he wanted to be allowed a fight.

'My thanks to the law, gentlemen, but *no*. Being an outlaw's not all it's cracked up to be. 'Specially when you're innocent. I'll stay put.'

He turned from the window, and looked

straight at Dan. 'Don't forget, you've an education to finish. And unless I'm mistaken, there's a pretty young filly in the stalls, keen and feisty.'

It was the kind of mush that troubled Dan. 'You'll get a chance to die with your boots on. We all will. Ham, give him his gun and a rifle, and stack those cartridges in the corner. Watch the rear door for Lem, when he comes. I'll take the front with Will. Rufus you take that side window.'

Dan looked around him at the doubtful faces. 'I'm the West Pointer, don't forget. Officer material.' He grinned, turned to the narrow window and spoke quietly into the street. 'We're taught how to do this.'

The four defenders of the jail took up their positions. Their guns were fully loaded, and extra ammunition was within reach. Dan and the marshal had their gunbelts, carried Winchesters, and had laid scatterguns at their feet.

An ominous silence filled the street, but now and again, they caught the waft of drunken courage from the River Bend Saloon. They pushed up the big desk to the front door, and waited for the inevitable.

After fifteen minutes, the sound of riders stirred them. A group of men rode at full speed past the jail, and Will levered a shell into the chamber of his rifle. 'That's some of 'em. Lummock's friends. Looks like Dobbs out front, and Charlie Chalk, the sumbitch.'

Dan squinted into the street. 'Yeah. Should have known. He was close to Cotton, wasn't he? I should have put him in here when Cotton was killed.'

It turned quiet, and they heard the sharp sounds of boots and spurs on the sidewalk. Someone banged loudly on the rear door of the jail, and Dorfmann let the deputy sheriff in.

Grange looked around the inside of the jail, and pulled another rifle from the gun rack. 'Won't be long now.' He thumbed shells into the magazine. 'Amazing what a quart of snake piss'll do to your head.'

Stone almost whispered, 'Here they

come.' He eased up the window, and pushed the barrel of his rifle across the sill.

The shouting and bravado increased, and the mob swung out from the sidewalk. They spilled into the street directly in front of the jail. One man, who appeared calmer and more set than the rest, placed a foot on the low wooden step. He pulled the rim of his hat down around his forehead.

Dan swayed away from the other window. 'Who the hell's that?'

Without looking Grange answered, 'The ramrod of the Bent Horn. Know him?'

Dan did. The hat made it difficult. It was the man whom Curly had pounded into the ground, out at Horse Creek.

Will turned to his brother. 'They shouldn't bunch like that. Wouldn't take more'n one of us to clear the herd. Like a tale of the old buffalo hunts. Do it with your eyes closed.'

Grange was peering through the window, over Stone's shoulder. 'I can see Dobbs. He's hanging back now. He's not taking any chances with *his* hide, eh, Will?'

Dan had a quick look across the street. 'Mr Dobbs thinks he's got a lot to live for.' He rolled away from the window with his back against the wall. 'Egg man's here.'

The butt of a gun banged loudly against the door, and egg man's voice called out, 'It's your brother we want, Sheriff. Send him out.'

Dan's spirit was pumping. 'Don't anybody move. I know what I'm doing. They won't shoot.' He shoved aside the desk, pulled the door open a foot, and stepped onto the walk. He faced up to egg man, who'd immediately stepped back into the street. The foreman's Colt was gripped tight in his hand. Too tight, Dan instinctively knew.

Shuffling uneasy behind the Bent Horn man, were a few of Lummock's friends and acquaintances. Dan lifted his rifle towards them. 'In the name of the law, I can order you men to disperse, but I'll make it simple.' He swung the rifle round, and pointed it behind him. 'That's county property, and the first man who tries to go in will die. If you all try, there'll be no one left standing. I'm the sheriff, believe me.'

They were the only words he could think of and, as he said them, he thought of Filena. She was right. Pompous, and he hated the job.

The egg man sneered. 'Nice speech, Sheriff. Nice an' tough.'

In the circumstances, Dan thought a touch bravely.

Egg man waved his Colt and turned to face the men backing him. 'We letting the kid back us all down? Come on, let's take the killer.'

From somewhere at the rear of the shifting mob a gun fired, and Dan felt a sting of air past his neck. He swore and ducked, as the blast of two scatterguns crashed from behind him. He spun back to the crowd, and levered off two bullets. He backed up the steps to the door of the jail and yelled, 'It'll be the bullets you want then?'

He sent off another two rounds into the

front of the mob, and saw men falter with cries of pain and anger. He caught sight of a man he once recognized before his face became a crimson pulp. There was a yell from Will, and someone dragged him back into the jail and slammed the door. As he sat on the floor, shaking, a deafening explosion of lead splintered the door frame and the window shutters above his head.

21

Some Live, Some Die

The jail was mainly clapboard; only the rear section which contained the cells was made of stone. No one ever had in mind such a ferocious and deadly barrage, and in a matter of seconds, the windows had been blasted away. Shards of wood and glass trashed the office, and the cells whined and pinged in the chaos of ricocheting bullets. But in the street there were a number of men flattening the dust. They were mostly wounded, but some lay dead. Some sought shelter, while others continued to pour heavy fire into the jail.

Stone and Will sat crouched behind the desk, Grange stood rigid, in back of the store-room, and Dorfmann had his hands clamped to his ears. Will rolled onto all fours, and looked across at his brother. 'They won't shoot, eh?'

Marshal Stone joined in. 'You'll never grow old as a sheriff, Sheriff.'

Dan crawled away from the front door. 'I don't aim to.'

Stone looked around the shattered room. 'This is what we're here for, boys. On the count of three, ready?'

As Stone called *three*, the defenders of the jail poured a fast and deadly stream of fire from the windows. They were heavily out-numbered, but they were more practised and expert, and Dan took out Swinton Dobbs with a deliberate shot. The would-be saloon owner had outlined himself against a window, and when Dan's bullet struck him, he did little more than stagger, before sinking slowly to his knees. Then he looked up, as though seeking a saviour. In the rictus of death, his hands gripped the pillar like an act of devotion.

Beneath Dobbs's feet was a lifeless testament to Rufus Stone's proficiency. Two other bodies, sprawled and awkward, one of them crawling and whimpering for help. To complete the deathly tableau, Will had accounted for at least four more. They weren't all dead, but three were very still, and templed in a heap. Above Dobbs, Charlie Chalk hung from the building's low eaves. He was hooked around a chimney stack, his thin legs hanging like twigs. Spread-eagled across a broken wagon-wheel, egg man, the ramrod of the Bent Horn, twitched convulsively, his toes kicking the ground, summoning a last angry frustration.

Stone yelled for them all to stop firing, and the men in the jail spun away from the windows. They sank to the floor, looking stunned at each other. The onslaught had been desperate, but the sudden quiet was almost as fearful. It filled the jail, mingling with the acrid bite of gunpowder. None of the men had their eye on the rear door of the jail, and none of them caught the movement as it crashed open. There was a loud, hollow bang, and Dan let out a grunt of pain. Instinctively he doubled up, but even before Will could reach him he'd straightened out and pumped another round into his Winchester.

'Just a graze, Brother, just a graze.'

Will swore, and looked across to where the marshal was sitting under the shattered remains of the window. 'You all right, Rufus?'

The marshal, as though looking for a rest, had dragged a chair from the store-room, but Will got no reaction from him. Stone was breathing, but not much else.

'Rufus is hit Dan,' Will shouted.

Dan mumbled something obscure, and his head was dipping. It was more than a graze, and Will could see the blood welling around the top of his brother's gunbelt. Will stood up, stepped to the front door of the jail, and grabbed the handle. Grange shouted, his voice cracking with fear.

'What the hell you doing, Will? Where you going?'

Will, looked calmly at the deputy. 'How many do you think's left out there, Lem? Half a dozen? There's two men dying in here, and one of 'em's my brother. No need for you and Ham to die. You shouldn't have to defend me any more.'

Dan was almost incapable of making a response, and before Grange or Dorfmann could try and stop him, Will yanked open the door. His voice was lost in the instant crash of gunfire. 'How good *are* you then?'

Dan groaned softly and crumpled into the floor. Grange and Dorfmann held Winchesters, and stood shoulder to shoulder in the doorway. They watched Will running pell-mell. It was dark, and bright flashes spouted from his Smith & Wesson. Bullets spat into the dust around his feet, and whined around his head like killer bees.

As Grange and Dorfmann pumped bullets into the dimly lit mob, they heard a strangled yell. The group of men turned back towards the jail. They were caught between a town marshal, a deputy sheriff, and Will Glass. The men scattered, hurling themselves frantically into cover along the sidewalks.

Hatless, and long hair flying, Will plunged through the mob at a gallop. He'd pulled a horse from the corral, and doubled back. He looped his arms around the horse's neck, and swung to the ground in front of the jail. He stepped onto the landing, and calmly levelled his gun between Grange's eyes. 'Now, go get a doctor before my brother dies.'

It was a fleeting command, and as Will waved back at the distraught pair, Grange said softly, 'I thought he was going to shoot me.'

Dorfmann looked at the deputy. 'I think he nearly did.' He motioned Grange into the jail. 'You look after them, and I'll get Heggarty. He can't be far away.'

By the time Dorfmanm had returned with the doc, Grange had lit more lamps, After a quick examination, Dan and Rufus were carried to the hotel, and a night of relative calm settled over Eagle Spring.

By morning, most of the carnage had been pulled or carried from the street. The marshal was looking after his recovery, and Dan was weak, but comfortable. As they lay in their beds, the marshal turned painfully to Dan. 'When this is over ... how long you gonna be sheriff?'

'Why, Rufus?'

'It's my retirement. I've been thinking about it.'

Dan turned his head slightly. 'What's that got to do with me?'

The old marshal groaned. 'Undertaker's job. As long as you're around, that's where the money is.' He closed his eyes. 'Regular too, ha ha.'

Filena Parker stepped quietly into the room. She looked at Stone, then sat next to Dan's bed. He still felt the bite of the last words she'd flung at him. He didn't want to, but he greeted her cautiously. 'The only time I see you, Filena, is when I'm on the backfoot. I don't remember ever being ahead.'

Filena chewed her bottom lip. 'Yes, sorry. It must seem like that.'

Dan held out his hand. 'Why do people always say they're sorry, when someone's lying in bed, close to death?'

She squeezed his fingertips until he felt discomfort. 'Perhaps this time, death will only come close.'

The door opened, and Heggarty looked into the room. Like Filena, he too glanced at Rufus, and then at Dan. 'Well, you're still in demand. You've got another visitor.'

Someone tapped lightly on the door, and Filena and Dan looked at each other. Then he came bustling in, fiddling with his hat in his hands, his eyes roving around the room. 'Will. We thought you'd run away again.'

Will grinned idiotically. 'Naah. I've had enough of that. I saw Judge Northwood this morning. Walt knew where I was. He came to tell me that you were all right. The judge says I haven't much to worry about. I don't know what he meant by that. I think it means they'll hang the warrants, not me.' He laughed, and looked at Filena and Rufus.

Dan looked wearily at his brother, then Hensa stepped cautiously through the open door. He smiled at Filena, and said hello, to Will. He looked firmly at Dan. 'The old stream bed. It's filling again. Not the torrent yet, but on the move. It'll be approaching Horse Creek.'

'How do you know, Hensa? Have you been there? You've seen it?'

'No. It was a group of the ranchers, with Deputy Grange. They climbed to the timberline at the old dam site. They went to have a look, to see for themselves. Well, those heavy rains from high in the peaks had cut another channel. Now there's two courses, and the water's taken the easiest route down. It now follows the old stream bed.' He looked back at Dan. 'It's the end of the fight I reckon.'

Daniel Glass was tired. He looked at the

faces around him. He had some mending, then some thinking to do. West Point, Filena Parker, Sheriff of Eagle Spring, his brother.

As he closed his eyes, everybody was looking at him. But none of them knew what he had in mind, or their part in it.

The publishers hope that this book has given you enjoyable reading. Large Print Books are especially designed to be as easy to see and hold as possible. If you wish a complete list of our books please ask at your local library or write directly to:

Dales Large Print Books
Magna House, Long Preston,
Skipton, North Yorkshire.
BD23 4ND

This Large Print Book for the partially sighted, who cannot read normal print, is published under the auspices of
THE ULVERSCROFT FOUNDATION